Lana waited. His eyes, so dark and unreadable, rested on her impassively.

Yet there was a tension in his gaze as well. As though, she thought, Salvatore might not continue with this exchange after all.

She sat still—she was used to doing so for extended periods during photoshoots—keeping her expression neutral. Then, abruptly, he spoke again.

"I find myself in a situation—" he drew a short breath "—that requires a certain...line of action."

The accented voice was brisk now, and very businesslike. The dark eyes were obsidian suddenly, the planed cheekbones taut, the sensual mouth a tight line. And the tips of his fingers around the cusps of the arms of his chair had discernibly whitened.

He's steeling himself—

Slowly, she was beginning to realize why, and a crease formed on her forehead. His next words gave the explanation bluntly, brusquely and blatantly.

"I wish," he said, "to discuss the possibility of a proposal of marriage between us."

Julia James lives in England and adores the peaceful verdant countryside and the wild shores of Cornwall. She also loves the Mediterranean— so rich in myth and history, with its sunbaked landscapes and olive groves, ancient ruins and azure seas. "The perfect setting for romance!" she says. "Rivaled only by the lush tropical heat of the Caribbean—palms swaying by a silver-sand beach lapped by turquoise waters... What more could lovers want?"

Books by Julia James

Harlequin Presents

Billionaire's Mediterranean Proposal
Irresistible Bargain with the Greek
The Greek's Duty-Bound Royal Bride
The Greek's Penniless Cinderella
Cinderella in the Boss's Palazzo
Cinderella's Baby Confession

One Night With Consequences

Heiress's Pregnancy Scandal

Visit the Author Profile page
at Harlequin.com for more titles.

Julia James

DESTITUTE UNTIL THE ITALIAN'S DIAMOND

Recycling programs
for this product may
not exist in your area.

ISBN-13: 978-1-335-73859-2

Destitute Until the Italian's Diamond

Copyright © 2022 by Julia James

For questions and comments about the quality of this book,
please contact us at CustomerService@Harlequin.com.

Harlequin Enterprises ULC
22 Adelaide St. West, 41st Floor
Toronto, Ontario M5H 4E3, Canada
www.Harlequin.com

Printed in U.S.A.

DESTITUTE UNTIL THE ITALIAN'S DIAMOND

To JW, my outgoing editor. Thank you for all your help and support over the years.

CHAPTER ONE

SALVATORE LUCHESI CAREFULLY eased his body away from that of the woman who was pressing ardently against him.

'Gia—no...' he began, keeping his voice temperate.

'Oh, Salva! Don't you *know* how crazy I am about you?'

The woman's voice was a mix of cajoling and demanding. She'd turned up uninvited at Salvatore's Rome apartment, pushing in impetuously on the grounds of long acquaintance, coaxed a cocktail from him and was now, quite literally, throwing herself at him.

Salvatore tried not to sigh heavily. *Si, Dio mio!* He most definitely knew how crazy Giavanna Fabrizzi was about him! But even if she hadn't been the daughter of his closest business associate, her dark, sultry beauty as much as her youth—she was barely twenty, if that—was not to his taste at all. His taste in women ran to cool, long-legged blondes.

They, he freely acknowledged, made a perfect foil for his own looks—tall for an Italian, but with the typical olive-toned skin and dark hair and eyes. Plus, he also acknowledged, without vanity, he had the blessing of a face arranged in features that women found highly attractive and a tautly honed body that men envied.

'Gia, *cara*,' he said now, stepping away from her to hold her at arm's length. 'I'm immensely flattered—what man wouldn't be? But you are Roberto's *daughter*—I'd be mad if I dared to mess around with you!'

He tried to keep his tone humorous. Gia was a pain, but she was also notoriously volatile—over-indulged by a doting father—and he did not want to trigger a scene.

Gia's almond-shaped eyes widened. 'I don't want an *affair* with you, Salva!' she cried.

Her scarlet mouth lifted yearningly to his, and Salvatore could feel her pushing forward against his restraining hold on her arms.

'I want much, much more!'

He stared down at her. A bad feeling was starting to form in the pit of his stomach, and at her next dramatic announcement he knew exactly why.

'And so does Papa! He's told me! And he's right—totally right! It would be perfect—absolutely perfect!' She gave a lavish sigh, lips parting as she gazed hungrily at him. 'I want to *marry* you!' she trilled.

The bad feeling in Salvatore's stomach turned to concrete.

Lana's feet hurt in their killer platform shoes as she stood in the wings with the other models, then, as her turn came, stalked out on to the runway to the pounding music. After ten years in the modelling business she could do these shows with her eyes shut.

Did I ever really think all this was glamorous and exciting? she thought with an inward sigh as she swivelled expertly at the end of the runway, hand on hip, holding her pose for the correct amount of time, before stalking back up again. She had once, years ago, but now, with twenty-seven looming, she wanted to call it quits finally.

Except that she could not afford to.

Tiredness lapped at her. She'd been working non-stop with photoshoots and back-to-back shows during this frenzied fashion week, and it wasn't over yet. There was still the after-party for the VIPs to get through, which all the models had to grace.

Some half an hour later she was doing the requisite mingling, wondering when she might be able to make her escape, knowing she had a heavy work schedule the next day. Helping herself to a glass of calorie-free mineral water, she glanced uninterestedly around at the wall-to-wall models, stylists, editors, all the glittering entourage of *haute couture*, clustering around the designer and his top assistants.

Male eyes were coming her way, but she took no notice. Her mouth tightened. The one time she had she'd made the biggest mistake of her life.

How could I have been so stupid? Letting Malcolm into my life.

Mal by name and *mal* by nature, she thought darkly. But she'd not seen it. Wanting only, she knew with a pang in her heart, someone—anyone!—in her life to stop her feeling so alone.

Bleakness fleeted in her eyes. That nightmare time,

nearly four years ago now, when both her parents had been killed in a motorway pile-up, had been unbearable. Letting Mal into her life had helped her bear it, helped her blot it out. And her eagerness to have someone had blinded her, she knew with hindsight, to Mal's character. She'd imagined he cared about her—but all he'd cared about was having a model as a trophy girlfriend, to make him look good as he grafted his way upwards as an aspiring actor.

Black fury replaced bleakness in her face. It turned out, though, that there was something else he'd cared about. The flat she'd bought in Notting Hill, paid for out of her savings from years in the modelling business and with what she'd inherited from her parents on their death. Mal had been very interested in that flat of hers…

She gave a mental shake. She was here to mingle, not to brood on Malcolm's perfidy. Resignedly, taking a sip of water, she glided forward again.

Salvatore accepted a glass of champagne from a passing server and took a brooding sip, looking with indifference at the party in full swing going on all around him. As an investor in the fashion house he'd been invited to the London show, but his mind was back in Rome. And the problem he faced there.

Gia—or rather, her father. Because Roberto, just as Gia had declared, saw things his spoilt daughter's way too.

'It's an ideal match!' Roberto had told him fulsomely. 'You couldn't ask for a more beautiful bride,' he'd said fondly. 'And I would be more than happy to entrust her to you, safe from fortune-hunters!' His eyes had narrowed. 'Do you have any objections to marrying my daughter?' he'd demanded, a discernible edge in his voice.

Salvatore had kept his face expressionless.

You mean apart from her being an over-indulged princess, nearly fifteen years younger than me?

'Any man would think themselves privileged to marry my Giavanna!' Roberto's eyes had narrowed again. 'You don't need me to tell you, Salvatore, how closely enmeshed we already are—so many joint ventures between us. Marriage to Giavanna would ensure they continue, make our partnership even closer.'

Salvatore's face had become even more expressionless. So that was what was behind this absurd notion! Well, his response would be adamant and ruthless, and then it would clearly be time for him and Roberto to end the business association that dated back to his father's days.

It could not happen instantly, however—there were ongoing ventures which either had to be completed, or from which Salvatore had to extricate himself without loss or complication. He did not want Roberto fighting him, or blocking him, by refusing to give up on the idea of his marrying his daughter. Somehow he had to convince Roberto it was a non-starter.

Making himself scarce had been the a first step— this impromptu visit to London and the fashion show… unnecessary but timely. He glanced around him, taking another brooding mouthful of champagne. But as he lowered his flute the mass of people parted, shifting his view. And into his sight came someone who stilled the glass in his hand.

Por Dio, but she was fantastic! Golden hair piled high, a racehorse figure robed in a skin-tight scarlet and crimson evening gown that slithered down her long, slender body and even longer legs. He could not take his eyes from her. The room was full of show-stopping women dressed to the nines. But there was something about this one—

His gaze lingered.

Bellissima...assolutamente bellissima...

The fulsome description fitted her perfectly. Perfect features, high cheekbones, wide-set eyes...and a mouth made for kissing.

He felt his hormones kick in and moved forward.

The blonde's head turned slightly and she saw him.

And she stilled completely.

Lana froze. A man was walking towards her. People stepped aside as he did so, and she knew why. Knew, too, why her pulse had suddenly given a kick—why her head had turned to let her eyes focus straight on him.

Tall—taller than herself—in a tuxedo whose jacket was set superbly across lean shoulders, dark-haired, dark-eyed, and with Latin looks that—

Take my breath away.

Chiselled features, mobile mouth, winged eyebrows over night-dark eyes. And with something about him that effortlessly radiated wealth and power.

A money man. One of those unseen backers of all this, whose money pays for all of us and who collects the profits we make for him.

But she didn't have time to think any more. Or to analyse. Or consider.

He'd stopped in front of her.

And suddenly, out of nowhere, there was no one else in the crowded room except him.

Salvatore stopped. His eyes had never left her. Up close she was even more spectacular. He could see the vivid green of her eyes, like jewelled emeralds—could see, too, with a kick of his hormones, that they had flared wide at his approach.

He lifted his glass of champagne to her.

'Don't tell me...' he said, and his voice was a drawl. He inserted an edge of humour into it. 'You're a model.'

For a second she did not respond. Then— 'Don't tell me,' she echoed. 'You're a money man.'

Deliberately she echoed his gesture too, lifting her glass to him.

Salvatore gave a laugh, short but genuine.

'Well, I'm certainly not one of the birds of paradise here—male or female!' he riposted.

He felt himself relax, settle into the exchange. His hormones were cruising along nicely, and in his head new thoughts were shaping. He could do with diverting them from the problem of Roberto and his pernicious pampered daughter. And this fantastic female here could divert them very, very easily...

'Tell me,' he said, relaxing his stance, wanting to engage her in conversation. 'How will this collection go down, do you think?'

She made a slight face. 'Word is two of the fashion editors here like it—the one from New York is less keen. But the Chinese guy is smiling, which everyone will like, because that market is massive. Which,' she said pointedly, 'you don't need me to tell you.'

'No, but it's good to hear you tell me that he's smiling,' Salvatore said.

It was good just to be in conversation with her. But it was a conversation that was not, to his annoyance, destined to last any longer. Someone was swooping down on him. One of his countrymen.

'Signor Luchesi! *Mi dispiace!* I did not see you there—'

Voluble Italian enveloped him, inviting him to join the exclusive circle around the celebrated designer. Impatiently Salvatore wanted to fob him off, return his attention to the breathtaking blonde, but she was drifting away—accepting, it seemed, that he'd been claimed by those a lot more important than herself.

He gave a half shrug of resignation, allowing himself to be ushered unctuously forward, a fresh glass of champagne pressed upon him. He'd catch up with the fabulous blonde later. He did not intend to let her slip through his fingers.

But some twenty minutes later, when he'd finally extricated himself from the circle around the designer, when his needle gaze threaded through the crowded room it drew a blank. Where had the fabulous blonde got to? A frown formed on his brow. She was nowhere to be seen.

Lana stood on the London pavement, under a bus shelter, relief at her escape from the after-party filling her. There was only one slight regret—if she could call it that.

That man—the money man who came over to chat me up...

Usually when she was hit on at these affairs she never engaged. But this time had been different.

Why?

She stared out into the damp chill night as the ceaseless traffic on the busy street went to and fro. An answer formed in her head and she couldn't dismiss it.

Because he was the most fantastic-looking guy I've seen in my life!

Nothing like Malcolm's blond beachboy look—she was off that look for ever! No, that money man tonight had a completely different appeal. Dark and devastating...

She felt again the kick that had gone through her as her eyes had met his, during the brief conversation they'd had.

Too brief.

She gave an inner sigh. It didn't matter how bowled over she'd been by him. He'd walked away and that was that. Besides, there was no point in wanting anything more from him. Not with her life in its current mess.

Wearily, she flexed her aching feet again, blessedly

in flats now. She was glad to be back in her own comfortable clothes, hair brushed out into a loose ponytail, her face clear of make-up. She looked down the street, hoping to see a bus approaching.

There was no sign of one.

Instead, gliding into the bus bay was a long, silver-grey expensive-looking saloon car. It was driven by a peaked-capped chauffeur, and the rear passenger door was opening on her side. A man in a tuxedo was half leaning out towards her.

'So,' said the lethal-looking Italian money man who'd zeroed in on her at the after-party before zeroing out again, 'there you are!'

His voice sounded deep, accented—and filled with satisfaction.

A kick went through Salvatore. It had annoyed him not to find the stunning blonde model again, and now here she was. He'd recognised her instantly, even with her hair tied back and wearing a trench coat. She was having exactly the same impact on him as when he'd first set eyes on her. And he definitely wanted more of it. More of her.

He undid his seat belt, getting out of the car. 'Why did you disappear?' he asked her.

His eyes raked her over. Yes, even without all the fancy clothes and coiffure and make-up, she was every bit as stunning as he'd known she would be. And his visceral response to her was every bit as strong.

She was replying to him now, giving a little shrug. 'I snuck off early,' she said.

He smiled. 'Good,' he said. 'Come and have dinner with me.'

A look of surprise crossed her face—and something more. Something that registered at an instinctive level of his masculinity. That increased his satisfaction.

But she was shaking her head. 'I'm calling it a day. Heading home. My feet are killing me.'

Was there regret in her voice? He was pretty sure there was.

He cupped a hand under her elbow. 'Then I'll give you a lift.' He glanced down the road. 'There's no sign of a bus, and you look cold. Besides, it's coming on to rain.'

For a second he felt her stiffen, and then, as a few drops of rain conveniently precipitated out of the murky sky, she let him usher her into his car.

'Where do I tell the driver?' he asked.

She gave an address—a quiet road in Notting Hill— and he relayed it to the chauffeur, who nodded behind his glass screen as he changed direction and set off to cross Hyde Park towards Bayswater Road, instead of heading towards Park Lane and Salvatore's hotel there.

'I hope it's not too out of your way—but you did offer!' The blonde's voice was half apologetic and half not.

'Not at all,' he assured her smoothly.

He smiled across at her. Her face was in chiaroscuro now, as the intermittent light from the street and passing vehicles played across it. He felt that kick go through him again, welcoming it.

'Will you change your mind about dinner?' He turned to look at her as the car moved off again into the traffic. 'There are some excellent restaurants in Notting Hill!' he said lightly.

She shook her head again, and he was surprised. Women did not usually turn down dinner invitations from him. His eyes rested on her appreciatively. In the time since he'd last set eyes on her she had not lost an iota of the impact she'd made on his senses. His eyelids drooped in sensual assessment.

'Thank you—but I really do need to head home.'

Her voice still sounded composed, but he suspected she was not as indifferent as she was making herself out to be.

He was glad of her turning him down now. Perhaps it made sense not to rush things with her. He'd acted on impulse in picking her up as he had, and that was unusual for him. Unusual to the point of his never doing so. His affairs were always carefully considered and of deliberately limited duration, and he chose the women he had them with just as carefully.

So why act on impulse with this stunning blonde?

The question flitted, but he dismissed it.

'Perhaps I could take you to dinner another evening,' he said now. He would happily extend his trip to London to do so.

For a moment she seemed to hesitate. Then she shook her head. This time he was sure there was regret in her face.

'I really can't afford any more complications in my life right now,' she answered.

He honed in on the key word. 'More?' he asked. She didn't answer and he pressed again, an unwelcome thought occurring to him. 'Are you involved with someone?'

If she were, then he definitely didn't want to have anything to do with her. But she shook her head—quite decisively.

'No—thank God! Not any longer!'

His eyes rested on her. He could see agitation in her face now.

'A broken heart?' he asked.

If so, that would be a definite no for him too. He preferred to keep things simple when it came to women—no complicated emotions ricocheting around.

'A broken bank balance!' came the retort. Anger flashed in her face, her voice. 'Courtesy of my ex-boyfriend! It means I have to work non-stop right now.' She looked at him square-on. 'I can't take any time out for…well, for dinner for a start. Or…' She didn't quite look at him now. 'Or for anything else.'

'I'm sorry to hear it,' he said smoothly.

He was, too. In this confined private space she was having a powerful effect on him, from the perfection of her profile to the gold of her hair.

'So am I,' he heard her say, almost *sotto voce*.

That made him speak again. 'What did your ex do to you?'

'He took out a four-hundred-thousand-pound mortgage on *my* flat!' she bit out. 'Then did a runner, leaving *me* to repay it!'

The anger was back in her voice, in her face, in her emerald flashing eyes.

Salvatore's eyebrows rose. For a woman without his

kind of financial background that was a hefty amount indeed.

She broke eye contact with him. 'I'm sorry. I don't know why I blurted that out,' she said tightly.

She looked out of the car window suddenly. They'd reached Notting Hill Gate and were heading down Kensington Park Road.

'Oh, I'm the next cross street after this one. On the left!' she exclaimed. The car was already turning, guided by the satnav, and drawing up outside a handsome plaster-faced house, part of a well-kept terrace.

Salvatore glanced at it. No wonder the ex had been able to raise such a hefty mortgage—property in this part of town did not come cheap.

As if reading his thoughts, she threw a look at him. 'Years of non-stop modelling, plus an inheritance,' she said, and anger was audible in her voice again. 'And the bastard's gone off with half of it!' She shook her head. 'I'm sorry,' she said again. 'I've got no call to dump any of my problems on you!'

Her voice changed and she undid her seat belt. The chauffeur was already opening her door for her.

She looked back at Salvatore as she started to get out. 'Look, thank you for the lift. I'm sorry about dinner, whether tonight or any other time, but…well…' Her voice trailed off and she just shook her head.

Did her eyes linger on him—was there regret in them if they did? But she was getting gracefully out of the car.

She glanced back in. 'I'll wish you goodnight,' she said, and now he was sure he could hear regret.

Well, he felt it too. For himself. He raised a hand in farewell. Should he ask her name? Give her his card?

But she was already crossing the pavement, running lightly up the steps to the glossy black front door, fetching a key out of her handbag. Then she was inside.

She hadn't looked back at him.

The chauffeur was back in the driver's seat, and Salvatore told him to head to his hotel. He would be dining in his suite…alone.

Che peccato.

A pity.

CHAPTER TWO

SALVATORE WAS BACK in Rome, having taken in an extended trip to New York and Chicago after London. He'd been half glad, half reluctant to leave London, and it was because of the fabulous blonde—the one he'd wanted from the moment of seeing her, but who'd told him she didn't have time for him.

Yes, well, he could see why…saddled with that crippling debt she was working all hours to service. He frowned a moment. Had she told him because she'd thought she could get *him* to pay it off for her? After all, he'd admitted to her he was a 'money man'—

He dismissed the suspicion. If his wealth *had* been of interest to her in that respect she'd have snapped at his invitation to dinner—at the possibility of having an affair with him.

He was glad he didn't have to think ill of her in that way. Even though it made it all the more frustrating that she had turned him down.

The phone rang on his desk and he snatched it up, glad of the distraction from thinking about a woman who didn't have time for him…even though he, he knew, would have made a considerable amount of time for someone that stunning and desirable…

But the voice on the line was a distraction he did not welcome. It was Roberto—pressing him to come to lunch. Ostensibly it was to discuss the progress on a joint venture they had both invested heavily in, but when—warily—Salvatore joined him, Roberto was soon back to pushing Giavanna at him.

'She needs an older man, my darling Giavanna… someone to guide her and protect her!'

'But that man, Roberto, cannot be me,' Salvatore retorted.

He could see a mulish expression forming on the other man's face—Roberto liked getting his own way. *Like father like daughter,* he thought cynically.

'Why?'

The challenge came bluntly. Demandingly. Belligerently.

Salvatore's irritation and annoyance turned to exasperation. He needed something that would stop Roberto in his tracks, yet not put his back up so much that he would make excessive trouble when Salvatore extricated himself financially from him. Something that would be impossible for Roberto to challenge. And only one thing occurred to him.

'Because…' he made his voice sound resolute '… I am involved with someone else right now. Someone,' he went on, hearing the words fall from his lips—hearing them with a disbelief that was echoed in Roberto's face as he spoke them. 'I intend to marry.'

The words were there, pulled out of thin air—and they could not be unsaid.

Just where they had come from Salvatore had not the faintest idea. Only he had a bad, bad feeling that he had just burnt every boat in his possession. And then some—

Lana climbed wearily aboard the bus. She'd been working non-stop all day—three shoots—and was fully booked for tomorrow as well. The following day was lighter—just a single casting. She frowned slightly—it was in an odd place, somewhere in the City. There had been no mention of the client, or what the campaign was, nor any other details. She'd agreed to it because she never turned work down these days. However exhausted and dispirited she was.

I can't go on like this—I'm burning myself out just keeping up with the sky-high interest payments.

Malcolm had not bothered to look for cheap borrowing. He'd simply applied for a mortgage on her behalf, using a fake email address he'd set up for her, brazenly forging her signature on the loan documents. He'd had the money paid into the joint bank account he'd persuaded her to open with him to make paying household bills easier—not that he'd ever paid any—then immediately transferred it to his own account and cleared out of her flat.

She'd come home from a foreign shoot to find him and all his stuff gone—and a letter from a completely unknown mortgage lender setting out just how much she owed them, and what the crippling rate of interest on the massive loan was.

As for Malcolm, probably living it up God knew where, on *her* money, he was untraceable. Her vociferous complaints to the mortgage company, her solicitor and the police had met with sympathy, but if there was no one to prosecute for apparent fraud—well, there was nothing that could be done except what she was doing—working herself to the bone, day after day.

She stared bleakly out of the bus window.

However hard I work, will I have to accept that the only way I can pay off this crippling mortgage is by selling up, taking a massive hit, and then finding some place outside London for half the price of what the flat is worth?

It was a galling prospect, and she felt familiar fury at Malcolm bite again. Her expression changed as she heard in her mind her own voice railing about him to that fabulous Italian who'd given her a lift home after the fashion show two weeks ago.

I just blurted it right out to that man—a complete stranger!

Yet there'd been something about him that had made her want to be upfront with him.

Maybe it's because after what Malcolm did to me— the lies, the deceit, defrauding me—I just want honesty.

After all, the fabulous Italian had been upfront about his invitation to her. Dinner, she knew perfectly well, would have been the first step towards an affair. An affair she just didn't have time for…and she'd been upfront about that straight off.

Her expression became rueful. The first man to have drawn her interest since Malcom had done the dirty on her, and she'd walked away...

But it hadn't stopped her thinking about him. In the four weeks since the fashion show she hadn't been able to forget him. During tedious shoots, holding her poses while photographers argued with stylists, his image—those amazing Latin looks, his dark, long-lashed eyes, his sculpted mouth—had constantly made its way into her head as she'd replayed her encounter with him. Replays laced, she knew, with something she had to admit was very much like regret...

Well, it was too late if so—he'd made no attempt to contact her again. Although he knew where she lived, and it would be easy enough for him to find out her name from her agency via the fashion house he was an investor in. But he hadn't.

A man that gorgeous—and that rich!—won't have to hang around waiting for a woman to say yes to him...

No, she'd missed her chance with him—and maybe that was just as well, given her unrelenting workload.

Wearily, Lana got out her phone and checked her appointments for the next day. Work: that was her priority—her sole agenda.

Nothing else.

And certainly not some drop-dead gorgeous Italian whom she would never see again...

Salvatore paced to the window of his serviced office suite in the City, from where he conducted his London business. He frowned. What he was contemplating right now was not business—

More like insanity!

He shook his head. No, it was *not* insanity! It was very real, very practical, and the more he went through the advantages, the more sense it made. Since making that impulsive, even desperate announcement to Roberto, to stop the damn man in his tracks—which it had, totally effectively—he'd gone through all the arguments, pros and cons, exhaustively, in a ruthlessly rational fashion. And he had come to one conclusion only. The cons could be limited—and managed—while the pros…

He felt a kick to his system. There was one very definite pro. And it had nothing to do with getting Giavanna and her father off his case and everything to do with the woman he had quite simply been unable to get out of his system. Just why, he still could not account for. It had been over a month since the fashion show, and surely that was time enough to forget all about her? Yet he hadn't.

And now—

The phone on his desk rang and he snatched it up.

She was here.

Lana followed the svelte secretary from the outer office of this very upmarket office suite in the City, still with no idea what she was turning up for. The brass plate at the entrance had simply said *Luchesi SpA*. Was it some Italian fashion house she'd never heard of?

As the secretary shut the door behind her, she took

in a large space with a lush dove-grey carpet, a pair of grey leather sofas and a huge mahogany desk—behind which someone was sitting.

She stopped dead, an audible exclamation breaking from her.

It was the drop-dead, lethal-looking Italian money man. The man she'd turned down for dinner—and anything else! The man whose image she had not been able to get out of her head—now here, right here in front of her.

He was getting to his feet. 'Thank you for coming. Won't you sit down?'

He indicated a leather and chrome chair in front of his desk, then resumed his own. Dark eyes rested on her, as unreadable as his expression, but still she was all too aware of their magnetic effect on her. She hadn't set eyes on him for weeks, but he still had an instant impact on her that she had never experienced before. She could feel her heart-rate increase, but managed, through long schooling, to keep her expression composed and inexpressive, saying nothing yet.

For a moment he just rested his gaze on her, giving nothing away but, she thought, both assessing her and taking stock. His manner, it dawned on her, was quite different from his relaxed demeanour at their first encounter. Now it was formal—businesslike.

Thoughts, confused and hectic, flashed through her mind.

Just what is going on? Because whatever it is, this isn't a casting!

'Before we proceed,' he was saying now, his English accented, as she remembered it, and the low timbre of his voice having the same effect on her now as it had that evening after the fashion show, 'I must ask you to sign this.'

He withdrew a piece of A4 paper from a leather folder on his desk, placed it in front of her. Lana's eyes dropped to it.

'It's an NDA—a non-disclosure agreement,' she was informed. 'What I am about to say to you must remain between ourselves only.'

Her eyes went from the paper to him, but his expression was still unreadable. She leant forward to skim-read the document—which did, indeed, seem to be nothing more drastic than an undertaking, legally binding, by her to make no reference in any way to any person or organisation or representative thereof, to any part or the whole of the content of the discourse about to take place, today or subsequently at any time, via any media, whether voice, written or electronic, et cetera, et cetera.

Her gaze went back to him. This was so different from their first encounter she could not make sense of it.

'Look, signor—' She halted, realising, with a start, that she had no idea who he was.

'Luchesi,' he supplied. 'Salvatore Luchesi.'

There was reserve in his voice, she could hear it. Almost, she recognised, a wariness.

'What is going on?' she asked bluntly. 'My booker told me this was a casting of sorts...'

A mordant expression was in his eyes. 'Of sorts,

yes,' he echoed, his reserve still apparent to her. 'If we proceed.'

For a moment he just surveyed her, with that unreadable look on his face. Then he placed a gold-tipped, very expensive fountain pen in front of her, nodding slightly at the NDA. She picked up the pen and signed. Clearly he would say nothing more until she did. She pushed the paper and the pen back towards him. He slid the signed and dated NDA back into its folder and rested his gaze on her again.

His expression was still unreadable, but something, Lana fancied, had changed within it. And across his broad shoulders, so elegantly clad in his bespoke suit—Milan, not Savile Row; she'd recognised that from the off with her practised eye for fashion—sat a new slight but discernible tension.

She waited. His eyes rested on her impassively—so dark, so unreadable, and so unfairly fringed with velvet lashes that, had they been fringing a female's eyes, would not need mascara to thicken them.

But there was tension in his gaze as well. As though, she thought, he might not continue with this exchange after all.

She sat still—she was used to doing so for extended periods during photoshoots—keeping her expression as neutral. Then, abruptly, he spoke again.

'I find myself in a situation…' he drew a short breath '…which requires a certain line of action.'

The accented voice was brisk now, and very businesslike. The dark eyes were obsidian, suddenly, the planed cheekbones taut, the sensual mouth a tight line.

And the tips of his fingers had discernibly whitened around the arms of his chair.

He's steeling himself.

The realisation was in her head, and a frown as she wondered why that should be so was starting to form on her forehead.

His next words gave the explanation. Bluntly, brusquely and blatantly.

'I wish,' he said, 'to discuss the possibility of a marriage between us.'

Salvatore heard the words fall from his own mouth. In that instant if he'd been able to recall them he would have.

Had he really, truly, gone and said them?

Yes, he must have. The look of extreme astonishment on her face told him so.

His own face set. Too late to backtrack now. He'd launched his bombshell and he must follow it through.

A tight, almost-smile pressed at his mouth. 'Yes, I agree—not what you were expecting,' he commented. He took a breath, deliberately slackening what had become an iron grip of his hands around his chair-arms. 'However, there are sound reasons—indeed, quite sane reasons—for what I have just said.'

She still hadn't moved, let alone replied, but instinctively he raised a hand as if to silence her.

'Hear me out,' he instructed.

For a second he gathered his thoughts. He'd rehearsed his argument countless times since the notion had first come to him, but now it was to be for real.

'I require,' he went on, 'at very short notice, a female in my life whom I can present, for a limited but immediate period, as my wife.'

He halted. She was staring at him as if he were mad, and he could well understand why. He lowered his raised hand and placed it palm down on his desk, pushing his chair back slightly, making himself adopt a more relaxed pose.

It wasn't one that was echoed in Lana—she was still sitting there, completely frozen, completely expressionless.

Yet still stunningly beautiful!

She was dressed in neutral colours: a pair of dark blue narrow-legged trousers, and a grey, close-fitting top with a loose but smart jacket worn over it. Her feet were in heels, but of modest height. Her hair was drawn back into a ponytail, and she wore only light make-up. But she was still far and away the most stunningly beautiful-looking female he had ever set eyes on—and she was having exactly the same impact on him as she had the first time he'd seen her at that after-party.

She refused me then—will she refuse me now?

He crushed down his reaction to her. Time for that later. For now, it was all about the reason he'd just dropped his bombshell in front of her.

He took a breath, short and indrawn, and made himself speak, keeping his voice impersonal, dispassionate. 'I have,' he began, 'a long-standing business partnership with an associate of my late father, who has recently taken it into his head that I...' his voice tightened '...would make a suitable husband for his daughter. A notion that, unfortunately, his daughter also shares. She, however…' and now his voice was edged '…would *not* make a suitable wife for me! And although I have tried hard to convince both herself and her father of that truth, neither is willing to accept it.' He took another incising breath, felt his jaw tense, his mouth thin. 'It has, therefore, become clear to me that I must…reluctantly…take drastic steps to dispose of a nuisance that has become increasingly irksome…to me. Hence,' he concluded, 'what I have just proposed to you.'

He fell silent, his gaze resting on her, still veiled. For a moment longer she did not move. Then she did.

She got to her feet.

'I'm sorry you went to the trouble of drawing up that NDA I just signed, *signor*, because it won't be necessary. I would *never* make any mention to anyone of this *insane* discussion!'

She made to turn, presumably to exit, but Salvatore was before her. He was on his feet, around his desk, blocking her way to the door.

'Unusual it might be—insane it is not,' he said tightly.

Her head swivelled. 'It's insane,' she insisted.

He didn't argue with her. He cut to the chase instead.

'Whatever you or I choose to call it, I am prepared, should you agree to spend the next twelve months as my wife, to pay you a sum that will entirely clear the outstanding debt your ex imposed upon you.'

His eyes met hers. His were unreadable. Hers were not. They had widened, and in them was a mixture of disbelief and something quite different.

Salvatore stepped away. Behind the mask of his expression he was giving nothing away. But he knew from long business experience that he had hooked her.

'Let us discuss this more fully,' he invited, and gestured to the pair of leather sofas.

Jerkily, but obediently, Lana did as he'd bade.

Relief filled Salvatore. And more than that—anticipation. But that was for later. For now there was the matter of a marriage to be hammered out…

Lana's head was reeling. Numbly, she sat herself down on one of the sofas, sinking down into its depths. Opposite her, on the other one, the man who had just offered, with a flick of his fingers, to lift her out of the bottomless financial pit Malcolm had so callously tossed her into did likewise, crossing one elegant leg over the other.

'What I require from you is this,' Salvatore Luchesi said.

He spoke in the brisk, impersonal tone he'd used since her arrival—which perhaps, she allowed, made it easier to cope with what he was saying…easier to forget that he'd once invited her to dinner, to an affair.

'As soon as it can be arranged, we will undertake a legal marriage. After which you will return with me to Rome, where we will present to the world the appearance that we are normal married couple, following a whirlwind romance here in London.' His voice tightened. 'A wife at my side will dispose once and for all with the wishes of my business associate's daughter and her father's ambitions for closer financial involvement with me. I shall use the duration of our marriage to extricate myself from my various complex high-value joint ventures with him. Once that is accomplished…' his eyes were holding hers, an intent expression in their dark depths '…our marriage can… and *will*…terminate.'

Lana said nothing, still trying to get her head around what he was saying. But he was speaking again.

'At that point we will divorce, and you will receive, according to the prenuptial agreement you will sign before we marry, the sum of four hundred thousand pounds and any accruing interest.'

She swallowed, her head still reeling, and fought to get control of her blitzed thoughts.

This isn't really a marriage—it's a business deal, that's all! A marriage for public consumption only. And when it's over I get my debt paid for me.

And because of that—because he was going to pay off her mortgage for her—of course the marriage would be for show only…nothing else.

Something flickered inside her as if it were a little dart, piercing her.

Nothing else.

Her own words echoed in her head, that little dart piercing again. At their first encounter he'd invited her to dinner—to an affair. She'd turned him down.

Now all he wants is a business deal.

A business deal that would lift the crushing burden of debt from her.

'Well?' The single word fell from Salvatore Luchesi's lips. 'Do we proceed?

For a timeless moment Lana could not answer.
Then she did.

Salvatore stood in front of the bathroom mirror in his
hotel suite, adjusting his bow tie, preparing to set off
for a livery company dinner in the City.

So he had done it. He had put into motion what
surely was the most extreme solution to his infuriating
predicament that he could possibly have come up with.

And yet—

His expression changed as he dropped his hands,
eyeballing his own reflection. And yet it had simultaneously achieved a very different goal.

Lana was everything he remembered about her
and more. Just as stunningly beautiful. He'd sounded
brusque, he knew, putting his proposal to her—but
he'd needed her to understand right from the off that
their marriage was going to be temporary only. Actual
marriage—real, lasting marriage—was not for him.

He stared at his reflection for a moment, eyes shadowing. He had his father's looks, he knew—but was
that all he'd inherited from him? Grimly, he suspected
not.

Transient affairs—that was his style. His preference.
He would not risk anything else.

With an abrupt movement, he turned away. Time to
head off for his dinner. And tomorrow he would press
ahead with expediting all that had to be done before he
could return to Rome—with Lana at his side.

CHAPTER THREE

LANA STOOD IN front of the registrar, supremely conscious of the man at her side. The man she was about to marry. All the paperwork had been completed—another, even more comprehensive NDA, and a rigorous prenup. Now there was just the wedding ceremony to get through.

Her eyes dropped to her ring finger and she swallowed. She had already known Salvatore Luchesi was rich—he was a money man, after all—but the glittering diamond-encrusted engagement ring he'd slid onto her finger just before they'd walked into the register office had made her widen her eyes.

'It will be expected that you wear a betrothal ring,' he'd told her.

His voice had been impersonal then and it was impersonal now, as he gave the expected responses to the registrar. Hers was as well. A feeling of unreality had come over Lana, and she clung to it. This was not, after all, she reminded herself yet again, a real marriage—so of course reality felt far, far away.

Whatever had passed between her and Salvatore

so briefly, so fleetingly that evening of the fashion show—weeks ago now—had been and gone. What they were undertaking now was reflected both in her own cool, calm composure and in the brisk, businesslike demeanour he was treating her with.

As she stood beside him now, with neither of them looking at each other, only at the registrar, she could catch the faint scent of an expensive aftershave—could feel against her own sleeve the slight brush of his. And she knew that if she turned her head even a fraction she would catch his distinctive profile, the sensual curve of his mouth, the high cheekbone, the sable hair, the strong line of his jaw.

But that was irrelevant.

As was the slight but discernible pang that went through her at the fact that it was so.

He wants nothing else—and I want...

Well, that was irrelevant too. The very nature of their marriage made it so.

That and that alone was what she must remember.

Salvatore picked up the leather-bound menu and tried to peruse its offerings. But his thoughts were on matters unrelated to lunch.

So, it was done. He'd entered into a state of legal marriage with a woman who was barely more than a stranger for reasons which he had resented being imposed upon him in the first place. But there was no point in rehashing all that now, when their signatures were on the marriage certificate.

His eyes lifted briefly to Lana as she sat opposite him, studying her menu with more attention than he was giving his. He felt his sombre mood lift discernibly and allowed his gaze to take in what he was seeing. She was dressed exactly right for the occasion, wearing a cream-coloured suit that accentuated her tall, racehorse figure, and wore her hair up, with a wisp of what looked halfway between a hat and a fascinator. The whole effect was dressy, but not specifically bridal. Only the diamond betrothal ring and the wedding band denoted her change in status since she'd got dressed that morning.

As did his own wedding band.

He could see the light catching at it, and memory slid uninvited into his head. His father had never shed his own wedding ring, however much he'd made a mockery of it.

He pulled his mind away from that thought. Silenced the thought that followed. That he, too, was making a mockery of the ring he was wearing...

Refutation was instant. No, he was not. Okay, so they'd married for reasons that people did not usually marry for, but the point was that they both had good reason to marry each other, and they both knew what that was. Their expectations of this marriage were the same.

Unlike his own parents'.

He silenced the memory again. It was neither relevant nor justified. He dropped his eyes to the menu again, making his choice, then glancing at the wine list.

Time to choose an appropriate champagne for the occasion. After all, he thought caustically, it was his wedding day.

Lana let her gaze rest lightly on the man sitting opposite her as he perused the wine list. He was totally at home in this quietly expensive restaurant in Knightsbridge, to which his chauffeured car had delivered them from the register office. Totally at home in a plutocratic lifestyle that was his birth right.

Luchesi SpA, she now knew, was a top player in Italian investment circles, or so it seemed, and had been so for close on a century. It had been founded by Salvatore Luchesi's grandfather, taken on to greater heights by his father, and now the man she had just married was expanding it even further.

But he didn't spend all his time on business, she had read. In her Internet searches about him his name had cropped up in the Italian tabloids and all the glossy magazines, There had been pictures of him attending glittering events on the Italian social scene—nearly always, Lana had not failed to notice, with a beautiful blonde on his arm.

And now it's going to be me.

It was a strange thought that now she was going to be paraded not just as his latest beautiful blonde, but as his chosen wife.

But not chosen for any reason that people usually choose who they marry. At heart, money is the reason both of us have married—Salvatore so he can extricate his financial affairs from a business partner he

*no longer wants, and me so I can extricate myself from
the mountain of debt Malcolm dumped on me.*

She realised the man she'd married for those pecu-
niary reasons was now asking her, in the same clipped,
brisk tones he'd used with her since his car had collected her and her luggage from her flat, what she
wanted to eat.

It was on her lips to order what she always ordered
in restaurants—grilled fish and undressed salad—
when it dawned on her, with an unexpected sense
of gratification, that for an entire year she'd have no
shoots or shows whatsoever. Not a single damn one.
She glanced at the menu again, her eyes falling to a
dish she had automatically ignored. She felt her mouth
water even at the thought.

She looked up at the waiter who had approached to
take their order. 'The chicken breast in marsala cream,'
she told him. 'With *pommes parmentier* and buttered
green beans.'

She closed the menu decisively as Salvatore gave
his own order, and then named the champagne he'd
selected. Lana felt her mood lift. There was a definite
upside to what she'd done—and it wasn't just because
of the mortgage she was going to be free of. She'd also
be free of her constant near-starvation diet. That was
a definite bonus.

Moments later, when the champagne arrived, she
all but thrust her glass out to be filled. Alcohol was a
calorific luxury in itself.

As the beaded bubbles blinked at her, gently fizz-
ing in the flute, and the waiter slipped away, Salvatore

raised his own glass. 'To a successful partnership,' he said.

His voice was still brisk, but there was something else in it too. A lighter tone. Slight, but discernible.

She lifted her lass, keen to taste the champagne. As she took a careful sip, savouring the soft mousse, a warning came to her.

All this is temporary—nothing more than that. Don't ever forget it.

It was a timely reminder. Everything about the life she had just stepped into was temporary.

Of their own volition her eyes flickered to the man opposite her, casually tasting the uber-expensive vintage champagne.

Including him.

As her eyes rested on him, on his looks as lethal as the rest of him, she knew with a slight tightening of the breath in her lungs that that was what she must remember most of all.

Salvatore heard the landing gear release and felt the plane move into its approach path to Fiumicino. Beside him in First Class his new bride sat, absorbed in looking out of the window.

'Have you been to Rome before?' he asked. It was something he would be expected to know about the woman he was going to present to the world as his new bride.

His mood darkened. In a very short while they would be in Rome, and the reality of what he'd done was hitting home. A woman who was all but a stranger was to be regarded by everyone as if she really was the woman he wanted to spend his life with—as if a whirlwind romance had indeed taken place. That was the fiction he had to make Giavanna and Roberto believe—and everyone else would have to believe it too. Including his friends. And his household. Everyone who knew him.

They'll believe a lie.

And, whilst he might not care over-deeply about what Giavanna and her father believed, it was different when it came to his friends, to those who knew him well…

Impatiently he pushed the unwelcome thought aside. What was done was done—now he just had to ensure it would work. And if that made him less than relaxed… well, so be it. The situation was inherently stressful, and that was all there was to it.

'A few times,' came the answer, and Lana turned her head to look at him as he addressed her. 'Fashion shoots. But I never have time to see the places I go to—just fly in and out.'

'Well, you'll have time now,' he replied. Briskly, he went on, 'We'll spend long enough here socialising to show you off—send the message to Giavanna and her father—and then I'll take you off to Tuscany, to the family *palazzo*. Officially we'll be on our honeymoon, so we won't have to entertain.'

The welcome thought lifted his mood. At the *palazzo* he could relax. They could both relax. And there, with Lana at his side, away from everyone else, with nothing to distract him, he could finally focus on her and her stunning beauty exclusively.

It was a pleasing prospect…

The stewardess was gliding by, inspecting their seat belts, interrupting his pleasing thoughts about life with Lana in Tuscany away from the world's eye.

Moments later the plane was on the ground, and shortly after that they were heading into Rome. During the drive he double-checked with his new bride just what she was to tell the people he introduced her to about how they had met and why they had married so precipitately. It was essential their story was convincing.

His eyes slid to Lana, sitting in the spacious passenger seat beside him, long legs elegantly slanted, her stunning beauty effortless in her well-cut wedding outfit, and he remembered how he'd given her a lift back to her flat after the fashion show party. She'd caught at his senses then, just as she was doing now.

His thoughts lingered a moment, then refocussed on what he still needed to tell her.

'We'll have this evening to ourselves, to allow you to settle in, but tomorrow we are lunching with friends of mine and I will introduce you then. That will serve to start the spread of the word.'

He gave her a brief rundown on them, and then moved on to the next essential item on his list.

'As my wife, you'll need a wardrobe to match your position, so use this time in Rome to go shopping.' His eyes glanced at her again in the passing streetlight now fitfully illuminating the car's spacious interior. 'You chose well for today,' he allowed.

'Thank you,' she answered evenly. 'It seemed to fit the bill. I've got something with me that I have in mind for lunch tomorrow. It's not this season—models don't get given those—but it's by an English designer, so not likely to be something your friends will have seen. Would that work?'

'I'm sure it will,' Salvatore replied.

His phone was ringing—the call was from New York and he needed to take it. At his side, his new bride turned her head, gazing out of the tinted window as they drove into the city. Salvatore left her to it, busy with his call, yet conscious that he would rather have gone on gazing at Lana's perfect profile...

Well, there would be time for that—he would make sure of it—but, alas, not right now.

With a mental shake of his head, he switched to business matters.

Lana looked about her appreciatively. Salvatore's apartment in the *centro storico*—the historic heart of central Rome—was huge: two floors at least of an elegant eighteenth-century townhouse set around a spacious interior courtyard. Inside the apartment, beyond the entrance hall, a double aspect drawing room stretched from end to end, overlooking the internal courtyard to one side and a peaceful-looking *piazza* on the other.

It was opulently but beautifully styled, Lana thought as she glanced in, with a mix of antique and more modern pieces. She had no time to take much in, though, as Salvatore was leading her towards another flight of stairs, less imposing than the external ones.

'The bedrooms are one floor above,' he said, as he headed purposefully ahead of her. Gaining the landing, her turned at the door immediately in front of him, which he then opened, flicking on the light. 'This is mine,' he informed her. 'Yours,' he went on, 'is next door. For obvious reasons that has to be so. There is a communicating door between the two.'

He headed for a door inset into the wall, opening it and gesturing for Lana to step through. She paused a moment to cast her eyes around the bedroom of the man whose wife she now was. It felt odd to do so. It was the first personal space of his she'd been into— a very masculine space, with huge pieces of antique furniture in heavy wood, dominated by a vast wood-framed bed with an intricate carved headboard.

Salvatore's bed—the bed he sleeps in...

Almost she could visualise him there...

Hurriedly, she withdrew her gaze, walking across to the open communicating door into the bedroom beyond. She stopped short, giving an exclamation of pleasure.

'Oh, how beautiful!'

She gazed around. It could not have been more different from the heavily masculine bedroom that belonged to Salvatore. Though just as large as his, this was a feminine space, the colour scheme of soft blue and silvery grey, the antique furniture light and graceful.

'It was my mother's room,' came the clipped reply to her exclamation.

She glanced at Salvatore, but his face was expressionless. Was it good that it had been his mother's room, or bad? She had no idea. And it was not her place to ask.

'What was once the powder room—in the eighteenth-century hair powder was applied in a separate room,' he was saying now, 'has been turned into an en suite bathroom.'

He strode to a door inset into the far wall, opening it slightly. Lana got a glimpse of a luxuriously appointed bathroom and abruptly felt the need to take off her shoes, and her constricting outfit, and stand under a refreshing shower after her long day.

My wedding day.

But the thought was impossible to compute. Okay, they'd said words, signed a register, but that hadn't been a wedding. Not a real one. Not one that actually *meant* anything.

Yes, well it does mean something, actually! It means I can get myself free of the crushing burden of debt that bloody Mal dumped on me! That's what it means!

Salvatore was speaking again, as cool and brisk as ever, saying that dinner would be served in forty-five minutes, and she should change into something more relaxed for the evening. He left her to it as a maid entered with her luggage, and Lana headed for the en suite bathroom to freshen up.

An air of complete bemusement took her over. She was here, in Rome, with a man she had married for a year and for four hundred thousand pounds—and it felt completely and utterly unreal.

*　*　*

Salvatore stood at his bedroom window, conscious of the ever-present hum of traffic in the ancient city coming from beyond the quiet *piazza* even at this midnight hour. Conscious, even more, of the woman in the bedroom next to his—separated from him only by a communicating door.

He was not sure what he was feeling. It was…complicated.

That same sense of the enormity of what he'd done that had struck him on the flight came again. Had he really done what he just had? *Married?*

He had the legal proof of it in the marriage licence now sitting on his tallboy, waiting to be filed under 'Personal' in his study. But *was* it personal?

The marriage bit was not—that was simply a means to an end in his business affairs. Separating Luchesi SpA from any involvement with Roberto Fabrizzi now that the latter had made a nuisance of himself.

But his bride?

She was 'personal'—definitely!

His mouth tightened. Except he would far rather, he knew perfectly well, she had remained 'personal' simply as the current woman he was interested in, the way her predecessors—and inevitable successors—had been or would be.

Not as my bride.

He gave a quick shake of his head, as if to dispel the word and the thoughts that went with it. Okay, so it might be complicated that the woman he wanted was also the woman he'd married for the reasons he had. But that was their only connection.

She is a woman I desire, who just happens, for now, to be the woman I have married.

That was not complicated—it was very simple. The way he liked life to be.

He turned away from the window. It had been a long day—and he'd thought about it quite enough for now. As he headed for his en suite bathroom his glance went to the thin communicating door on the opposite side of his bedroom.

Lana was on the other side.

For now, she would stay there. There were things that had to be done before that door could open.

One last thought flickered in his head.

She's in my mother's bedroom. My poor, unhappy mother—

He banished the thought from his head, firmly closing his bathroom door. Leaving the past behind.

Lana paused at the head of the staircase on the landing outside her bedroom. Dinner last night had passed easily enough, though an air of reserve had still emanated from Salvatore, as it had over lunch and their flight out to Rome. Now they were about to set off to meet his friends for lunch.

Nerves plucked at Lana fractionally as she walked down the stairs. Not because she was going to be on show—she was well used to that—but because of the role she had been cast in.

Salvatore Luchesi's bride.

Her task was simple—make his friends believe her to be just that. Well, she would do her best. No point having nerves of any kind. She would just do what she had to do—what, after all, when it came right down to it, she was being paid to do.

Salvatore was waiting for her in the entrance hall and she was all too conscious of his presence there. He looked, as he always did, a knock-out, in another hand-tailored suit, pale grey this time, and radiated the kind of effortless style that seemed to come naturally to all Italians, male or female.

Hopefully, though, she could hold her own. Certainly as she came up to him she saw approval in his eyes sweeping over her.

'You have chosen well—again,' he said, and there was slightly less reserve in his voice.

His dark eyes flicked over her once more, taking in the soft grey jersey dress that draped with deceptive ease over her tall frame, looking both simultaneously understated and eye-catchingly chic.

She was reassured by his praise, but then he frowned. She'd accessorised the dress with a heavy necklace of large haematite beads, but these, apparently, met with his displeasure.

'Wear these instead,' he instructed, fetching a large flat box from a nearby pier table and clicking it open.

Lana's eyes widened. 'Oh, how beautiful!' she exclaimed. 'And absolutely perfect for this outfit!'

It was a necklace of huge coin-flat baroque pearls and a matching bracelet. The price tag would have had a large number of zeroes on it, she knew, having modelled—under strict security conditions—enough expensive jewellery in her time. And modelling this fantastic necklace and bracelet was all she was doing now, she reminded herself, as she removed her own beads. Part of the role she was playing.

'Turn around...'

A moment later she felt the pearls move around her in a long loop, and then cool fingers were at the nape of her neck, fastening the necklace. It was only a moment—the merest snap of a clasp and a safety chain—yet something had been done to her nerve-endings in the sensitive exposure of her skin to Salvatore's touch. It echoed even after he stepped away, subjecting her to a critical appraisal, and then, with a nod of apparent approval, he handed her the matching bracelet to fasten around her wrist herself.

'Okay, let's go,' he announced.

Lana found herself glancing at him. There had been an audible tension in the brief command. Did he think she wouldn't pass muster with his friends? Eat peas off her knife? Make embarrassing remarks? Surely not.

Even so, she felt a flicker of unease go through her. She was about to be put in front of people he'd told her were long-standing friends, and they were meant to think that a whirlwind romance had so enthralled him that he'd married her on the spot. Wasn't that deceiving? She gave a mental shrug. Well, it was not her responsibility. She would just act her part, play her role to the best of her ability—what else could she do?

She put aside her faint unease, and headed off with him.

Lunch, so he'd already told her, was to be at the famed Viscari Roma, and when they arrived they were shown into a *salon privé* off the main dining room. Inside, four pairs of eyes snapped to her.

Keeping her expression carefully schooled, Lana let Salvatore guide her forward. Swiftly, she took in what was facing her.

The two men were not as tall as Salvatore, but they were both ludicrously good-looking in dark Italian style. The two women were quite unalike. One was an extremely pretty blonde, with a slight figure, a lot of make-up and short hair, wearing a sunshine-yellow outfit which Lana immediately recognised as the work of one of Italy's glitziest designers. The other female was taller, a long-haired brunette with a full figure, wearing a closely fitting dress that showed it to best advantage.

Salvatore greeted them all in laconic Italian. The note of tension in his voice was gone now. She heard her name mentioned—but only her first name. The man who was with the blonde returned the greeting first. Lana couldn't follow what he said, but she could certainly read the look in his eyes as his glance went towards her with well-practised masculine appreciation.

He came towards them, hand outstretched. Automatically Lana offered hers, and was not that surprised when it was lifted to his lips and kissed with a gesture that was part clearly exaggerated and part sending a definite message.

But not to her. He dropped her hand and said something to Salvatore in a low, throwaway voice that held a wealth of masculine appreciation.

'Thank you, Luc,' came Salvatore's dryly sardonic reply—in English. 'Your vote of approval means everything to me.'

Luc Dinardi—their host, as Lana knew from Salvatore's briefing—gave a low laugh, not in the least put out.

Now the other man was coming forward, also with a hand outstretched. This time, though, Lana's hand was not subjected to any practised Latin Lothario treatment, but simply a brief but firm handshake.

'Vito di Vincenzo,' he introduced himself, speaking English. 'And my wife, Laura.'

The full-figured woman stepped forward, her smile friendly. 'Hello,' she said. 'How lovely to meet you.'

Her English was perfect, and Lana quickly realised she was a compatriot.

Then the blonde was surging forward, her brown eyes alight. 'You look absolutely *fantastic*!' she exclaimed enthusiastically, her English highly accented. 'You absolutely *must* tell me who the designer is! Of course, only someone with your height could get away with it!'

Her bright eyes danced.

'We had no idea Salva was bringing his latest! And there's no need for him to tell us anything about you— you're a model! You just scream it!'

She gave an insouciant laugh and ran on unstoppably.

'Come and get a drink and tell me all about how you and Salva come to be together! I absolutely *adore* gossip and I want to be the first with this! How long has this been going on…when did you meet, and how…and what are you going to be doing in Rome now you're here?'

'Don't let Stephanie drown you with her chatter,' said Luc, the blonde's partner, humour in his voice. 'As you'll have realised, she never lets anyone reply anyway!'

The blonde exclaimed something in indignant Italian, as Luc enquired what Lana would like to drink, indicating the wide choice. Lana was about to give her usual answer of sparkling mineral water, when she abruptly changed her mind, remembering afresh that her starvation diet days were over.

'Sweet vermouth spritzer, please,' she said.

Luc busied himself mixing it for her, and Lana found Laura beside her. The blonde had zoomed up to Salvatore, to interrogate him.

'Don't mind Steph,' Laura said in a low voice, with a smile in her voice. 'She's completely harmless, but…' there was a slight warning in her grey-blue eyes '… she means what she says about loving gossip! And she adores passing it on.'

'I'll bear that in mind,' Lana said. 'Not that there is anything about me to cause gossip. Yes, I am a model— it's a bit of a giveaway when you're my height with my thinness.'

Even as she spoke Lana felt conscious that she was being disingenuous. In fact, there was a whole heap about her presence in Rome with Salvatore that would make explosive gossip. But there could not be a breath of suspicion about it…

'Not to mention the show-stopping looks!' Laura was saying now, smiling as Luc handed Lana her cocktail. She smiled back at Laura, liking her, and feeling again uncomfortably conscious of the deception being practised upon her...upon all of Salvatore's friends. She was falsely here as his wife. But there was nothing she could do about it except go along with it as best she could.

She took an appreciative sip from her drink as Salvatore came up to her. He was smiling at her, but she could see a watchful look at the back of his eyes. He addressed Laura, asking after her little boy. Lana saw the other woman's expression soften.

'That's a fatal question to ask me, Salva,' she said warmly. 'I can go on for hours about just how perfect he is!'

He laughed, and Lana took the opportunity to ask how old her son was.

'Three, going on four, and he is just *adorable*!' Laura enthused. 'I only hope that when—' She broke off, her glance going to her husband. 'Vito, shall we...?'

Her husband came up to her, put his arm around her waist. 'Let's,' he said. He held up his glass. 'My friends, now that Salva has joined us this is the perfect moment to tell you all that Laura and I are hoping to present our perfect son with a perfect brother or sister!'

He'd spoken in Italian, but Lana knew enough to understand what he'd said. Everyone promptly burst into hearty congratulations. Stephanie was particularly voluble in hers, rushing up to Laura to kiss her cheek and exclaim excitedly. Lana felt her elbow taken, and she was guided slightly aside by Salvatore.

'You followed that?' he asked in a low voice, and she gave a quick nod. In the same low voice he went on. 'I won't steal Vito and Laura's thunder right now, but when we sit down I'll make our announcement, so be prepared. No one seems to have noticed the ring on your finger,' he said dryly, 'or mine.' He paused, his expression changing, 'But that is not surprising... Stephanie's absolutely right. You do look totally fantastic.'

'Well, that was the intention,' Lana answered evenly, but the admiring way Salvatore had spoken made her nerves flutter. Then she realised she had better get used to praise and admiration from him—after all, she was his brand-new bride, and it would be expected of him. In public, anyway.

She turned back to Laura. 'What wonderful news for you,' she said warmly to the other Englishwoman.

Laura's smile was warm in return. 'Yes, it is. We're thrilled!'

'How many weeks are you?' Lana asked.

'Just gone twelve, so just into my second trimester now. Because I'm Junoesque—as my dear grandmother used to tell me!—I've got away with it so far.' She glanced at Lana's racehorse figure. 'I hate to tell you this...' she shook her head humorously '...but you won't ever get away with hiding even the tiniest baby bump!'

'Not a chance,' Lana agreed with rueful good humour. She didn't mind the observation—becoming a mother was so far off in her future that it was unimaginable. She felt herself frown. Not even with Mal had she ever once contemplated having a baby...

Maybe that should have told me something about him and what he meant to me. Or, more to the point, what he didn't mean to me...

It was something she knew she had to be grateful for. As she had blurted out to Salvatore that night he'd given her a lift home, all Malcolm had broken was her bank balance—not her heart.

And I don't want my heart broken—not ever.

She must take care that it did not happen. That she did not fall for a man who did not return her feelings. Who did not want to make his life with her.

Unconsciously, her glance went to Salvatore—the man she had married yesterday morning. Married for reasons that had nothing to do with the true purpose of marriage, which was to unite two people, two lives, in love for the rest of their lives.

Yet again, that feeling of unease went through her, She had married not just under false pretences, but for a reason that marriage should not ever be for. For money.

She shook the thought from her, glad of Salvatore's interjection now.

'Lana, we're taking our seats,' he told her, indicating the table in the centre of the room.

She took her place beside him, opposite Vito and Laura, with Luc and Stephanie, as host and hostess, at either end. A pair of waiters sashayed in, one with wine and the other with their *primos*. Lana felt her appetite quicken at the herby aroma coming from the buttered scallops in front of her. They proved every bit as delicious as they looked, and she ate with unalloyed pleasure, the delicious dish complimented with a fruity white wine.

'Are you one of those unbearable women who can eat anything she likes and it never shows?' Stephanie asked with cheerful envy. 'I only have to *look* at a plate of pasta and I get a kilo heavier!'

Lana shook her head. 'Alas, no. I do have to watch every calorie—or rather I did while I was modelling. That's why I'm so glad I don't have to any longer, now that—'

She stopped abruptly. Horrified. Then, suddenly, she felt her hand being pressed, such that she released her fork. Salvatore, at her side, was raising his other hand.

'I, too, have something to announce,' he said.

Lana felt his long fingers slide into hers on the damask tablecloth. It was a strange feeling, but she had no time to pay attention to the sensation as he went on speaking—in English for her benefit, she knew.

'For you who know me so well, this will come as a surprise—even a shock…' His voice was dry. 'But when I introduced Lana I failed to do so completely.' He paused—for dramatic effect, Lana was pretty sure. 'I now make good that omission. May I therefore ask you to raise your glasses—to Signora Luchesi?'

For a moment longer than the one that had greeted her entrance there was complete silence. Predictably, it was Stephanie who broke first. A squeal—just about a shriek, Lana thought—of over-the-top excitement burst from her. Then there was a cacophony of voluble Italian all around the table.

Lana felt Salvatore's hands mesh more tightly with his.

'We neither of us wanted a fuss made,' he was saying, still in English. 'It was a register office in London yesterday. I wanted you four to know first. Stephanie?' Salvatore's tone of voice was openly, if good-humouredly, pointed. 'I rely on you to tell all of Rome!' He glanced across at Laura and Vito, reverting to Italian. 'I never intended to steal your thunder, you two, so I hope you will forgive me.'

Vito threw up his hands. 'Of course! My God, I can't believe it Salva! You've always been totally allergic to marriage! Understandably, I know. But—'

Then he was being ruthlessly interrupted by Stephanie, who was beside herself with excitement. 'Salva, this is incredible! Just incredible! Tell us *everything*!'

Her eyes were alight, and it seemed to Lana she meant what she'd said. Fortunately, from the far end of the table, Luc spoke.

'Steph, my treasure, believe me. Salva and Lana are *not* going to regale you with the tale of their romance, let alone the details that you would sell your soul for!'

He spoke humorously, but with resignation in his voice. Then he picked up his glass, looking at Lana and then Salvatore.

'Every happiness in the world to you both!' he said.

This was echoed all around the table, most volubly by Stephanie, still visibly bubbling. Lana felt as if she was the opposite, sitting motionless next to Salvatore, who was taking it all in his stride.

Well, of course he is. That's what this is all about. Telling Rome—telling Giavanna and her father—that Salvatore Luchesi is now a married man, thank you, and off the menu.

And even as she reminded herself of the blunt truth behind the announcement she felt a sliver of…if not guilt, precisely, then definitely that sense of discomfort again. These people were genuine friends of Salvatore—their ease with each other, their familiarity, the warmth of their welcome to her all showed her that. Yet he was deceiving them. Making them believe that he had made a genuine marriage yesterday, however much out of the blue.

But it's just fake. Not real. Not genuine. A show. A deceit—

She tried to shake the sense of discomfort from her to tell herself that the deceit was all on his part, not hers. That she was nothing to do with it…that she was just doing what she was as if it were a business arrangement, nothing personal at all.

But the unease remained. Strengthened, if anything, during the course of the meal. For herself, Lana kept conversation to the bare minimum, especially with Stephanie, simply saying that she and Salvatore had met in London at an after-party, that it had been a whirlwind romance, and that that, really, was that. There really was nothing more to say.

Stephanie rolled her eyes in frustration. 'Well, at

least tell us where you are going on honeymoon! The Caribbean, the Maldives, the South Seas…?'

'Tuscany,' Salvatore answered decisively, and Stephanie made a disgusted face at such a tame destination.

'Your *palazzo* in Tuscany sounds more than gorgeous enough for a honeymoon.' Lana smiled at her husband.

She made her voice warm, though it felt odd to do so. Oddly intimate. Or perhaps it was the word 'honeymoon' that did that…

Well, obviously it's not actually going to be a honeymoon! It's just a place to stash me after showing me off here in Rome to get the message home that he is off the menu for Giavanna!

'Salva's place is definitely gorgeous,' Laura was saying. 'Do you know Tuscany at all?'

Lana shook her head. The conversation became general again, as they talked about Tuscany and all its cornucopia of cultural treasures, and Lana was glad. Glad, too, when lunch finally ended, well into the afternoon, and the party dispersed, with a lot of hugging and kissing and invitations all round for her and Salvatore when they came back from Tuscany.

As Lana got into the car waiting at the kerb, the same disquieting sense of discomfort about the deceit she was being a party to assailed her. Everyone had been so nice, so friendly, believing her to be their friend's real wife. It did not sit well with her.

Roundly, she admonished herself.

Well, you'd better damn well get used to it! It's going to last an entire year! That's how long you've got to fake this marriage for! And if you make any slip-ups you can kiss goodbye to your four-hundred-thousand-pound payoff at the end!

That was, after all, why she had married Salvatore. Not for any other reason.

Any other reason was impossible...

CHAPTER FOUR

SALVATORE SHUT HIMSELF into his study in his apartment, settling down at the antique desk that had once been his father's. Out of long habit his mind skittered away from the memories it held, focussing instead on the main problem currently facing him.

Tonight he was taking Lana to a charity fundraiser being held at one of Rome's grandest High Renaissance villas, situated on one of the city's famous seven hills. It was going to be a full-on affair where everyone who mattered would turn out to see and be seen—including Roberto and his daughter.

He'd had an evening gown delivered to Lana that afternoon, from one of Rome's most expensive couture boutiques, together with a diamond parure extracted from the bank vault. She would look every inch Signora Luchesi.

His expression flickered a moment. The last time those diamonds had been worn by a Signora Luchesi—worn at all, in fact—it had been his mother wearing them...

He felt his thoughts skitter away again, as they had

from the memory of his father sitting in this very room, at this very desk.

They were gone, both of them, his mother and his father. For a moment—just a moment—he found himself wondering what his parents would have thought of what he had done…marrying a stranger for the reasons he had. His mouth twisted. His father would have approved his choice of blonde bombshell. His mother—

He stopped his thoughts. He knew what his mother would have thought, and he didn't want to hear her voice in his head.

But he heard it all the same.

'Love, Salvatore my darling boy—only marry for love. Love shared and reciprocated! Promise me that—oh, promise me that!'

With a sudden bleakness in his face he reached for his pen, flicking open the file in front of him, ready to make his annotations to the documents printed out within.

Love was the last reason he'd married for. The last reason he ever would.

His mother should have known that.

Lana blinked at the brilliance of the scene in front of her. White marble nymphs framed the periphery of the room, completely unable to compete with their living female counterparts thronging the centre. Fortunately a lot less flesh was being revealed by the female guests than the marble nymphs were displaying, and as for the male guests—they were the usual army of strictly black and white penguins.

Not that the man at her side could ever be castigated in such a way. She'd only seen Salvatore in a tuxedo once before, the very first evening she'd met him, and when she'd seen him again as she'd walked down the stairs to the entrance hall of his apartment the sight had all but taken her breath away.

He really was quite magnificent in evening dress that was superbly cut and tailored to make the absolute most of his height and lean masculinity, and she found herself wondering, yet again, just what it was about dinner jackets, dress shirts, bow ties and winged collars that made all men look so…so fantastic…

But, as she glanced around the throng in front of her now, she knew without a doubt that the man at her side was the most fantastic-looking of all the males here.

Not that it mattered, of course, she reminded herself. He was not here to look fantastic for her—*she* was here to look fantastic for *him*.

And she did, she knew. Around her throat she could feel the heavy diamonds enhancing the ivory silk gown she was wearing, one shoulder bare, the bodice very plain, cut straight across her cleavage, then falling in soft folds to her ankles. Already she could see eyes turning to her as Salvatore guided her forward, hand under her elbow, greeting people to left and right as they made their way towards their hosts.

Then Salvatore was halting in front of a very well upholstered woman in late middle age, with a portly man beside her.

'Duchessa…' Salvatore was taking the proffered hand, kissing it with graceful formality, then shaking the outstretched hand of the portly man, a brief man-to-man gesture, before turning to Lana. 'Duchessa.' He spoke again, in English. 'May I have the honour of presenting to you my bride?'

Lana could see astonishment fill the matron's eyes, but she was too well-bred to do anything other than offer Lana her beringed hand and murmur something that was appropriate on such an occasion—some form of felicitation in accented English.

'Thank you,' Lana said, letting slip the Duchess's hand before repeating the gesture with the Duke.

Salvatore was telling her that he had the honour of presenting to her the historic owners of the grand villa, their hosts for the evening, complete with their high-ranking title, and she was smiling politely. The Duchess said something directly to Salvatore in Italian, which Lana could not follow, and Salvatore replied with a polite smile.

All Lana caught was 'London' and 'private wedding'. She kept her polite smile on her face and then they were moving on, into the throng. From then on, as Salvatore duly introduced her to all he spoke to, she got the distinct feeling that a ripple was passing through the guests. Heads were turning towards her, and she could hear Salvatore's name being uttered. Even though she did not follow Italian, she could tell it was with surprise and astonishment.

For herself, she did not turn her head at all, merely sailed forward with Salvatore, smiling politely, apparently unaware of the attention she was garnering.

Then, abruptly, their progress was halted. A middle-aged man and a much younger female at his side, newly arrived, were in front of them. Lana did not need an arrow over their heads to tell her who they were. She felt Salvatore's hand on her elbow tighten momentarily, but that was the only sign he gave.

He held out his hand. 'Roberto,' he said expansively, shaking the other man's automatically lifted hand. Then, dropping both the man's hand and Lana's elbow, he stepped forward towards the young woman at Roberto Fabrizzi's side.

Very young, Lana saw instantly, despite the full face of make-up and the over-sophisticated fuchsia-pink gown she was wearing by a Milanese designer notable for his opulence and extravagance. Although it suited the girl's darkly luscious looks, it was far too overpowering for her, making her look older than a girl who Lana was pretty sure was barely out of her teenage years, if that. Her full glass of champagne did not add any aura of sophistication either.

'Giavanna,' she heard Salvatore say, his voice fondly warm and with an avuncular tone to it that surely the teenager would detect. He went on in the same tone, his hands resting lightly on the girl's shoulders as if inspecting her. 'How spectacular you look!'

Even Lana could understand that in Italian, and she could hear the indulgent amusement in Salvatore's praise, almost as if she could hear him add *You look almost quite grown-up!*—which he tactfully did not.

But Giavanna's face was not displaying any pleasure at Salvatore's praise. Instead, she shrugged her shoulders free and glared at him. The expression, Lana thought, made her look a mere sixteen…or younger.

'You were going to bring *me* here, Salva!' she accused him. 'I *told* you Papa and I were coming—we were to arrive together! It was all arranged!'

'Only by you, Gia,' Salvatore said. The fond note was still in his voice, but with a slight tinge of reproof. He glanced at Roberto. 'I did let you know, Roberto, that I would be coming here almost directly from London. Speaking of which—'

Lana heard him say something briefly about what she presumed were his business affairs in England, catching one or two references to banks and so forth. It was as if he were giving the other man a swift report on business, she realised, to emphasise what held the two together. Business. Not Roberto's voluptuous but demanding teenage daughter.

As Salvatore addressed Roberto, Gia turned her attention to Lana. If the glare she'd subjected Salvatore to had been open, the one she arrowed at Lana was positively slaying. Something sharp came out of the girl's mouth which Lana did not understand. She merely smiled.

'I'm so sorry, I don't speak Italian,' she said in English.

The girl swapped to the same language. 'I just said that you shouldn't get ideas about Salvatore! He has a new blonde on his arm every month!'

'Oh?' said Lana temporisingly. Then, quite deliberately, with a smile that she kept polite, if not quite pitying, she said, 'I don't think that will be the case now.'

She lifted her left hand to rest on the diamonds at her throat, both indicating her wearing of them—very obviously a family heirloom—and letting the matching bracelet on her wrist and the diamond betrothal ring catch the light…the light that also caught the wedding band on her finger.

She saw Giavanna's expression change. It was now one of mingled horror, disbelief—and fury.

'It isn't *true*!' she spat, first in Italian, then in English. 'I heard someone say it, but I knew it wasn't true! It isn't true—it *isn't*!' She reverted to her native language, giving vent to her emotions.

Lana could hear a rising note not just of fury but of outrage, even hysteria. She saw heads turn towards them. Knew, with female instinct, that Giavanna Fabrizzi was not the kind to shy away from creating a scene when she felt like it. Already her father was saying something in Italian to her, his tone placatory and embarrassed.

Then Salvatore was speaking, cutting through Giavanna's dangerously rising tirade. 'Gia, I have done my best to convince you that I would make you the worst of husbands!'

He was speaking in English—presumably, Lana thought, so she would know what he was saying to the petulant girl. He was keeping his tone light, Lana could hear, but there was an implacable note beneath all the same.

'I am very fond of you—you are like my favourite niece, if I had one. And one day you will make a man the proudest in the world to call you his bride! But that day is not yet. Enjoy to the full these carefree days of being single, of slaying hearts wherever you go...'

Lana could hear the humour deliberately infused into the equally deliberate flattery.

'Enjoy your life before you settle down to the dullness of married life, keeping house, having babies. You are young, spectacularly beautiful, and you have the world at your feet! So—*enjoy*!'

He swapped to Italian, saying something to Roberto in a low voice. He nodded tightly. The older man's face was closed, and hard, and Lana did not like the expression in it. But it wasn't her business. Her business was to play the role allotted to her. So she went on standing there in a statuesque fashion, with a sympathetic look on her face, but nothing more than that.

Eventually Salvatore took her elbow again, and she knew he wanted them to move on. But suddenly, and quite viciously, Giavanna spat a word at Lana in Italian. It was coarse, and ugly, though Lana had no idea what the girl had just called her. A second later she had no more time to ponder. She felt a sudden cold splash on her face and neck and realised, in a moment of disbelief, that Giavanna had thrown the contents of her champagne flute all over her.

A sharp expletive broke from Salvatore. Even Roberto looked shocked. Lana could only blink away the beads of champagne on her mascaraed eyelashes.

A moment later Salvatore was handing her a silk handkerchief from his jacket pocket, and she was dabbing at her wet cheeks as best she could. She heard Giavanna say something in an angry, sulky voice, and gathered she was refusing to express even the slightest regret for what she'd just said and done. Lana was vividly aware that now heads were definitely turning in her direction, with shocked expressions on their faces.

Salvatore was saying something to her, but she waved her free hand. 'It's nothing,' she said dismissively. 'Champagne never stains, and the dress has caught very little of it.' She dabbed at the top of her bodice, then paid more attention to the necklace. 'I think these diamonds can withstand a little bath!' she said lightly. She turned to Salvatore. 'I'll just slip to the powder room to retouch,' she told him. 'Any idea where it is?'

He collared a server and made the enquiry, then pointed in the requisite direction.

'Thank you,' said Lana, using the same light tone.

She would minimise the incident—not just out of instinct, but out of an awareness that playing it down was the best thing to do. Already heads were turning away, and she was glad of it.

Squeezing the now damp silk handkerchief in one hand, she made her way to the ladies' room, gaining its privacy with relief. Bringing relief, too, a glance at her reflection showed that very little damage had been done. Her cheeks were splashed, eyelashes dewed, and a frond or two from her elegant upswept hair style were damp, but that was all.

Five minutes later she re-emerged, cheeks and diamonds dry, mascara and lipstick retouched, looking immaculate again. Salvatore was waiting for her outside in the quiet corridor leading to the powder room.

'I'm sorry about that,' he said stiffly. 'I didn't think she'd react quite that badly.'

'A teenager thwarted in love is unpredictable,' Lana said dryly. She handed him the rinsed out, wrung out silk handkerchief. 'I dried this as best I could with the hand drier, but it's a little damp still, I'm afraid, and very crumpled.'

He took it, stuffing it into his trouser pocket. 'Let's get out of here,' he said abruptly. 'The Duchessa will understand—'

Lana raised her eyebrows. 'So soon? Won't it look as if we've cut and run? Better surely to go back and show everyone how little it all meant?'

She spoke instinctively, forgetting for a moment that she was really no more than an employee of Salvatore Luchesi, and that she was there to do as she was told, not have ideas of her own, let alone express something contrary to him.

'Can you face it?' he asked, a frown on his face.

She gave an exaggerated roll of her eyes. 'If you had ever been backstage at a fashion show, you would know that Giavanna Fabrizzi's little outburst back there was a mere pinprick! I have seen full-blown hissy fits that would have given Mount Etna a run for its money when it comes to volcanic eruptions!'

She felt herself take Salvatore's arm, draping her hand over its smooth sleeve.

'Come on,' she said lightly. 'Show some backbone! I know men *hate* scenes—even Italian men, I dare say, though they probably see a lot more of them than

Englishmen are subjected to in high society—but you can do this!'

Unconsciously—instinctively, even—she made her tone humorous. There was a darkness in Salvatore's eyes that might have been forbidding, but she would not let it be. And now the darkness changed to a glint.

'Stiff upper lip?' he contributed sardonically, but she could hear humour, reluctant though it was, in his voice.

'I'm sure the Duchessa will insist!' she answered, still lightly.

They walked back into the throng. It felt slightly odd not to have Salvatore's insistently guiding hand cupping her elbow, and instead feel the muscle of his forearm beneath her hand. And as they walked the Duchessa herself was gliding towards them, very much a ship in full sail, guests parting on either side to allow her approach.

'My dear, are you all right?' she asked concernedly.

'Perfectly, I promise you,' Lana assured her.

'Bene, bene...' intoned the Duchessa. She bestowed an approving smile upon Lana. 'Well done!' The look she threw at Salvatore was less approving. 'Your bride should not have been subject to that kind of thing!' she said tartly.

Lana intervened. 'Young love is so very painful, Duchessa,' she said. 'Salvatore's marriage must have come as a deep shock to the poor girl.' Her voice became sympathetic. 'She has such a huge teenage crush on Salva!'

'You are too kind to her,' came the Duchessa's still tart reply. 'She's been over-indulged and spoilt!'

'I'm sure she'll improve as she grows up,' Lana said temporisingly. She wanted the subject changed. 'This is the most spectacular villa, Duchessa—it is a privilege to be here. The ceiling alone…'

She gazed upwards. As if on cue the Duchessa gave the name of the artist, and told her what the opulent scenes depicted by way of pagan gods and goddesses disporting themselves. Then she smiled at Lana.

'Come and lunch with me here one day, my dear, and I will be able to give you far more time than I can now.' The Duchess smiled benignly upon Lana, included Salvatore within it, and then she was sailing off again to attend to her other guests.

Lana felt Salvatore's hand fold over hers on his sleeve. 'You've found favour,' he said in a low voice. She could hear approval in it. Then something changed in his expression. 'I've announced you to the world—and to Giavanna and Roberto—as my bride. But perhaps…' Now his voice was changing as well. 'Perhaps I should give them a tangible demonstration of that fact.'

Before she realised what was happening—before she could even register his intention—Lana felt his hand catch her chin. He took a step towards her, closed the distance between them. His long fingers tilted up her face towards him, and her eyes, uplifted also, met his full-on.

Met them—and reeled.

They were dark, long-lashed, and drowningly deep…

And she was drowning in them…she absolutely was… Helpless to break his gaze, helpless to step away, helpless to do anything at all except know, with every female instinct in her, what was coming next.

And come it did.

As if in slow motion, Salvatore's sculpted mouth lowered to hers. His long fingers grazed the line of her jaw as his mouth touched hers. Lana's eyes fluttered shut, and sensation took over from vision.

Like velvet, like silk, like satin…

The sheer, blissful sensuousness of his mouth moving slowly, lingeringly on hers weakened every bone in her body. Did a sigh escape her? She did not know… could not tell. Could tell only that she did not want his kiss to stop. Did not want it ever to stop—

And yet it did. He was drawing away from her, his fingers releasing her, his hand dropping away. He was still close to her, though, so very close… The scent of his expensive aftershave was catching at her, making her feel faint.

Or something was…

Lana's eyes fluttered open to meet, once more, that drowning gaze, that gold glinting in the depths of his dark, dark eyes, pouring into hers. The rest of the world—the people in the room, the noise and the conversation—all had vanished. All gone. All that existed was his golden glinting eyes pouring into hers…

Her senses were reeling, the blood soaring in her veins. Her heart like a caged bird, beating wildly.

For one long, timeless moment she just went on gazing up at him. Helpless to do anything else at all.

And then—

A smile indented his mouth.

A smile of satisfaction.

'Well,' Salvatore said, and there was satisfaction in his voice, in his smile, in the gold glint of his eyes, 'I think we have just demonstrated very adequately that you are, indeed, my chosen bride.'

He tucked her hand into his arm, a proprietorial and masculine gesture, still smiling down at her. The rest of the world reappeared. The women in their couture gowns...the men in their dashing black and white tuxedos. The animated chatter echoed off the high painted ceiling and the marble floor. All of it snapped back into existence, despite the reeling of her senses, the wild beating of her heart...

'Time to circulate,' he said.

He reached to lift a glass of champagne from a passing server, handing it to her. She took it nervelessly and he helped himself to one for himself as well. Her blood was still whirling in her veins, her heart still a wildly beating caged bird. Her lips still echoed with his kiss...

Urgently, she tried to banish those lingering echoes. Suppress the rush in her veins. Rationalise what had just happened. Find an explanation for it.

The only possible explanation.

It was for show! It was just for show! He said it was—and that's all it was! For show—just for show!

She heard the words like a litany, playing urgently in her head, repeating themselves as, with a slight pressure on her hand, he led them both forward, resuming his greeting of people he knew.

Were they smiling at them both, smiling at the newlyweds, smiling at having seen them kiss like that? She didn't know, couldn't tell—couldn't do anything at all except let herself be taken where Salvatore wanted to go, standing at his side while in her head those urgent words kept sounding.

Just for show! Nothing else at all!

That was what she had to keep telling herself all the time they stayed in Rome. Keep telling herself that she was glad—relieved!—that the man she had married for reasons that had absolutely nothing to do with the way she had reacted to being in his arms would make no further 'tangible demonstrations' that required his kissing her.

After all, given the truth about their marriage, what else could she possibly be but relieved? It was the only appropriate reaction. Now all she needed to do was forget it had ever happened…

Something that, to her disquiet, she was finding disturbingly difficult…

Well, I just have to try harder then, don't I? she remonstrated with herself roundly as she stood, gazing sightlessly out of the window of her bedroom, trying not to remember the blissful sensation of his mouth moving on hers…

Trying, above all, not to let her eyes go to the communicating door. All that separated her from the man she had married.

All? The single word sounded silently in her head. She shook her head. No, much more separated them.

Much more.

With an impatient, resolute shake of her head she turned away from the window, padding to the bed in her jade satin pyjamas and tucking herself into its wide depths. She must get to sleep. Tomorrow they were leaving Rome, after a week of non-stop socialising, heading for Tuscany. It was a long drive, Salvatore had warned her, necessitating an early start.

The world would think them heading off on their honeymoon. But Lana knew better. Honeymoons were for real brides.

And she was not one of those.

CHAPTER FIVE

SALVATORE EASED BACK in the driving seat, increased the throttle, and felt the familiar and always satisfying power of the superb performance of the car—an exclusive model from an exclusive Italian marque. Also satisfying was looking back on the week in Rome that had just passed.

Despite the second thoughts about what he was doing that had assailed him on their arrival, the reality had proved his tension unnecessary. It had gone well—triumphantly so. Achieving just what he'd intended. Announcing to the world—to Giavanna and her father—that Salvatore Luchesi was no longer a single man.

And achieving more than that, too.

His expression changed and his glance went fleetingly to the woman sitting in the passenger seat, absorbed, so it seemed, by looking out at the passing scenery and countryside as they drove towards Tuscany.

Lana had been surprisingly forbearing about Giavanna's outrageous behaviour at the Duchessa's fundraiser. And, he acknowledged, she had been wise to do so. Rome loved nothing more than scandal to feast on, and the tale of how Giavanna Fabrizzi had hurled a glass of champagne over his bride would have lost nothing in the retelling. Everyone liked a tasty morsel of gossip. Had Lana reacted with outrage and hysteria it would have made the situation ten times worse! But her cool dismissal, playing down the incident and writing it off with a show of sympathy for 'teenage passion' had, he admitted freely, been masterly.

He threw another glance at her. He could only see her profile, as she was still gazing interestedly out over the passing countryside. But her averted profile was as beautiful and elegant as her full profile or her full face. She was, it seemed, incapable of looking anything other than breathtakingly beautiful, with her finely carved features, striking looks and those amazing green eyes of hers…

Memory pierced him. Those emerald eyes gazing up at him, seemingly helpless to break away. His hand tilting her face to his. His mouth descending on those perfect lips of hers, tasting their sweetness. Like softest silk beneath his own.

Oh, it had been for show, all right, that kiss—but also more than that. Much more.

Anticipation rose in him. Rome had been full-on, every day spent socialising, with no time for each other at all. But now—ah, now it would be different. In the privacy of his *palazzo* he would have this most beautiful woman all to himself, away from gazing eyes.

Away from all eyes but his.

He allowed himself the luxury of one last glance

at her profile, noting yet again its absolute perfection. Then he dragged his gaze back to the autostrada. It wasn't wise to feast his eyes on her—not while he was driving.

Not yet.

But soon—enticingly soon.

The prospect was very pleasing.

His good mood increased and he accelerated towards their destination. His breathtakingly beautiful bride beside him.

Lana's eyes widened—it was impossible that they should not. They'd just driven through a pair of impressive gilded iron gates set in a curtain wall, and crunched down a long, curving drive set between tall, pointed cedars, slowing down as Salvatore's Tuscan *palazzo* came into view.

Her breath caught. It was magnificent! It was as if she'd stepped into a historical drama and at any moment people in full eighteenth-century rig would issue forth from the massive carved oak doors set in the centre of the golden stone frontage, with its huge sash windows and a balustrade around the roof.

'Oh, my word!' she breathed, her gaze riveted.

The massive front doors opened as Salvatore drew up, and an elderly, august-looking personage stepped through, followed by a middle-aged woman dressed in black.

'Giuseppe is steward here—he has been with the family many years. The housekeeper is Signora Guardi, and other staff will become familiar to you in due course,' Salvatore was murmuring. 'Remember,' he said, glancing back at her warningly, 'they will treat you as the new mistress, but as they know how to run everything here to perfection, if they should consult you on any matter leave it to their discretion.'

Lana did not need reminding, and as she got out of the low-slung car she kept her expression guarded. Salvatore was welcomed with a benign greeting from Giuseppe and a respectful nod of the head from Signora Guardi. Then Salvatore was introducing her to them. She smiled, but stayed mindful both of her role and Salvatore's warning. She might appear to be the chatelaine of this stately pile, but in reality she was no such thing.

Then he was taking her elbow, guiding her inside. The interior of the *palazzo* was as impressive as the exterior, with a wide, pilastered, marble-floored hall, off which a series of double-doored rooms opened on either side. At the far end was a double flight of stairs arcing around to both sides, leading to the upper floor.

Her bedroom, so it seemed, had been created to look out over the rear gardens, set with three windows and furnished with beautifully painted and stencilled white wood pieces, including a huge bed covered in an exquisitely embroidered white silk quilt. The walls were a very pale eau-de-nil, with the same delicate floral stencilling around the ceiling's edge. Two crystal chandeliers hung from the ceiling, the lustres echoed in table and bedside lamps.

Lana gazed around with open pleasure as a man-servant brought in her luggage—which had been plentifully added to in Rome after several sorties to the designer boutiques of the Via dei Condotti at Salvatore's behest. A maid was hovering, waiting to unpack. Lana let her do so, while she freshened up in the surprisingly modern en suite bathroom. When she emerged it was to hear the maid informing her politely that she was awaited downstairs.

Obediently, Lana headed down, to be ushered into a room opening off the long statue-lined central hall. It was a dining room, high-ceilinged and imposing, with oil paintings on the walls, but the long, polished mahogany table was not set for lunch. She was shown through French windows to a wide terrace beyond. There, under the shade of a huge sail-like parasol, a glass and iron table had been placed, laid for lunch, and Salvatore was standing beside it.

For once, however, Lana did not have eyes for him—only for the vista in front of her. They were, it seemed, to one side of the *palazzo*, and the gardens beyond the wide terrace were sunken, reached by a set of stone steps and dominated by a large ornamental stone pond, in the centre of which was a sculpted fountain trickling water. Potted bay trees and olive trees were around the perimeter, the whole space girded by a sun-baked wall. Several carved benches were dotted about, each flanked by smaller bays and olives. It was both ornate and minimalist in its impact.

'The fountain is only turned on occasionally, to conserve water,' Lana heard Salvatore say.

'It's absolutely beautiful,' she said, taking the chair

he was pulling back for her and seating himself at the head. 'As is the whole place!'

'It was mostly my mother's creation—both the gardens and the interior,' Salvatore told her. 'She spent a great deal of time here. My father was usually elsewhere.'

Lana glanced at him. There had been a tightness in his voice she had not missed. It dawned on her that it was there whenever he happened to mention his parents, whether to her or anyone else. She wondered why. It was sad that it should be so.

She found herself wondering more about him, and the family he came from. He was one of Italy's richest men, moving in elite circles, with a historic *palazzo* to call home, and yet—

Her own childhood and youth had been so happy, with loving, warm parents—not rich, but owning their own house, sufficiently comfortably off, and so proud of their beautiful daughter becoming a successful model in a cutthroat world. Their tragic, untimely death had devastated her.

Making me vulnerable to Malcom—blinding me to his true nature. To the reason for his interest in me.

Her eyes went to Salvatore again as she shook a fine linen napkin out across her lap. She felt a flutter in her veins. He was nothing like Malcolm in looks.

Nor in nature, either. He's not devious or deceptive—he's completely up front with me about the reasons we've got married.

Mutual benefit. With the emphasis on mutual. Unlike Malcolm—

Darkly, she dismissed the man who had defrauded her. Stolen from her. She would not waste time thinking about him at all. Instead she would focus on the present.

Her gaze went to the two manservants, one of whom she recognised from the Rome apartment, who were now issuing forward with trays holding plates of a variety of salads. It all looked fresh and delicious, and Lana felt immediately hungry. She helped herself to a generous serving of leaves, plump tomatoes, cold chicken and a good dollop of oil-rich dressing and tucked in, savouring the taste. One of the menservants had poured wine, and she took a mouthful of the crisp white, savouring that too.

'You're definitely not eating like a model any longer,' Salvatore observed.

That momentary tightness as he'd mentioned his parents was gone. There was, she thought, a genial note to his tone of voice now. She looked across at him. Since setting out from Rome he seemed, she realised, to have set aside the reserved formality which she'd got used to when they were alone together.

In public he might smile at her, keep her close at his side—kiss her, even!—but that was only for public consumption. She sheared her mind away. Remembering that kiss was *not* a good idea! She'd been doing her very best to put it out of her head ever since it had happened, knowing perfectly well why he'd done it— he'd said as much to her straight out, after all. The two of them might as well be actors on a stage. In a way, they were—the glittering stage of Roman high society.

With the key members of the audience he'd wanted to see the kiss being Giavanna and her father.

That was the only reason he kissed me.

There was absolutely nothing personal about it. How could there be?

You turned him down, remember? The first time you met him. Said no to his invitation. What you have now with him is a business arrangement—nothing more and nothing less. And there are implications that follow on from that. Implications you must not forget. Must not ignore.

She realised, with a mental start, that Salvatore's eyes were still resting on her, and that she should answer his remark. It was a safe subject, so she did so freely.

'Do you know?' she declared, cutting into the soft chicken breast with enthusiasm. 'I almost think this is the best thing about all this. Eating my fill after years of starvation. It's bliss!'

Salvatore smiled. 'But won't you have to starve all over again when you go back to modelling afterwards?'

'I'm not going back,' Lana replied. 'That is definite. I'm past my sell-by in modelling anyway. Once I can pay off that damn mortgage Mal saddled me with I'm selling up completely and getting out of London!'

'Where will you go?'

She wondered why he was in the least interested in what would happen to her once she no longer had to stand at his side and pretend to be his wife, but then she reckoned he was just making polite conversation.

'I'm not sure,' she answered, tucking in with a will

to her delicious dressing-drenched salad. 'The seaside, probably, on the south coast. I might buy a place I can run as a holiday let, or maybe open a dress shop—that might be an idea.'

'I get the dress shop idea, given your experience of the fashion world, but why the seaside?'

Again, Lana wondered idly why he was bothering to ask, but since he had, she answered him. 'Childhood memories, really, from when I was much younger than now. Holidays with my parents. Until—' She stopped. It was still painful to think of them.

Dark eyes rested on her. She knew he was expecting something more after the sudden way she'd fallen silent. Too late to wish she hadn't mentioned them.

'They were killed in a motorway pile-up four years ago,' she said.

She swallowed, aware that he was taking a mouthful of his wine, then setting his glass down with a click.

'That's hard. To lose both at once.' His voice was short. 'Mine,' he said tightly, 'were killed when their private plane crashed off Sardinia. Twelve years ago now, but—' He stopped.

For a moment their eyes met. Something passed between them. Something that was nothing to do with the reason she was here in his beautiful *palazzo*, acting out being his wife when in truth she was no such thing. Something that was just between the two of them. Both with tragic memories.

'The pain stays,' Lana said quietly. She reached for her own wine, needing it suddenly.

'Yes.'

His voice was still tight. Lana knew why perfectly well. It seemed strange that both of them should have lost their parents in such similarly tragic and untimely ways. It seemed to link them, when in fact there was nothing linking them at all. Nothing personal.

Setting down her wine glass, she resumed eating. So did Salvatore. Was the silence between them awkward, or the opposite? She wasn't sure—knew only that it was safer to return to easier subjects.

'So, how old is the *palazzo*?' she heard herself asking. Her tone was conversational now, and that seemed safer, too.

He answered in kind, and that was better. 'Nearly three hundred years old,' he said. 'The family who originally built it sold it after the Napoleonic wars, and it changed hands again before my own family bought it.'

'May I explore?' she asked.

He frowned, as if her question were out of place. 'Of course. Unfortunately, I don't have time to show you around this afternoon—I must get some work done after my week of socialising in Rome. If you consider the weather warm enough, you might like to sit out by the pool—it's heated at this time of year, until summer arrives in full strength.'

'Thank you—that sounds very inviting,' Lana replied. 'What is our schedule for the time we'll spend here?' she asked. He'd set their schedule out in Rome, so she might as well discover what was expected of her here.

'As I say, I have a great deal of work to catch up with,

but I see no reason why I should not show you something of the area. Would you like that? You mentioned you had never been to Florence, for example. Would that be of interest to you?'

'Well, yes,' she agreed, 'but I can easily visit on my own. Please do not feel obliged to—'

'Lana.' He cut across her. 'We are supposed to be on our honeymoon—newlyweds! What new bride goes off sightseeing on her own?'

'I simply don't want to make demands on you,' she replied.

'You won't,' he assured. 'I'll show you Florence, and there is so much more, of course. Pisa, Lucca, Sienna—the list goes on and on! Even after a year you won't have seen all that Tuscany offers.'

His mood seemed to lighten again, and he started to talk about Tuscany. Lana asked appropriate questions about its geography and history, just as if she were an invited guest, and it made the meal pass pleasantly.

As the staff emerged to clear the table, he got to his feet. 'I must go and get some work done,' he said. 'Have coffee out here, or down by the pool if you prefer. Feel free to do as you please this afternoon—pool, gardens, house, whatever. Dinner is at eight, but we'll gather at half-seven for drinks. Dress code is informal—I want to be comfortable after a week of tuxedos!'

He strode off back indoors, and Lana's eyes followed him. Moments later the two manservants had gone too, taking her request for coffee with them, and she was left sitting on her own. There was no sound except birdsong. It was very peaceful. Very beautiful. She looked out over the sunken garden with the stone fountain, its water playing gently, bathed in warm sunlight.

I could get used to this....

And not just to the lifestyle. Her thoughts flickered. She found herself wishing, as she had before, that the man she had married to lift the crushing burden of debt off her shoulders had been short, fat and old. It would have made things a lot, lot easier...

Her gaze flicked to the chair Salvatore had just been occupying. She saw him there again, his powerful frame dominating her vision, the chiselled planes of his face, the dark glance of his gaze on her.

She felt sudden heat beat up into her.

Heat that should not be there. That had no place being there.

Salvatore clicked off his computer and pushed the keyboard away. He was done for today. Time for something much more enjoyable.

An enquiry of Giuseppe confirmed that Lana was out by the pool. Ideal...

He headed out.

The warm air after the cool of his office was welcome. Though it was still spring, summer was on its way. He strode across the terrace, making his way past the rear of the *palazzo* where, to the right, the pool court was situated, sheltered in a walled garden that mirrored the sunken fountain garden on the other side of the *palazzo*.

He vaulted lightly down the steps, through the archway towards the aqua of the pool's water, sparkling in the late afternoon sunshine.

And stopped dead.

He'd known Lana would be there, but—

She was lying spreadeagled, face-down on a lounger, completely naked apart from a skimpy bikini bottom, her glorious hair like a swathe of shining gold waving over one shoulder. His eyes swept over her—over her long, bare body, the fabulous moulding of her shoulders and back, the soft round of her barely covered derriere and the long, slightly parted length of her thighs and legs.

Desire, strong and insistent, swept instantly over him.

Slowly, deliberately, with nothing whatsoever else in his mind, everything wiped out by the vision in front of him, he walked towards her.

Lana stirred. She'd been dozing on and off, conscious dimly of the sun's rays, stronger here than this time of year in England, and knowing that she must not overdo her first tanning session. But after the non-stop week in Rome simply lying here, lazy and resting, in this quiet, peaceful spot, with nothing more than birdsong and cicadas to accompany her, the faint hum of the water filter lapping the water gently, was just so blissful she simply didn't want to move.

Yet something had roused her. Had it been footsteps? Perhaps one of the maids who had earlier brought her out some iced juice and then water at her request, as well as rich, fragrant coffee, had returned to remove the empties.

She lifted her face slightly to see.

And froze.

It was not a servant. It was Salvatore. Standing a handful of metres away from her and looking straight at her.

She knew exactly what he was seeing. Just about every square inch of her! And if she moved in the slightest, let alone sat up or turned over, he would see even more.

And he was enjoying the view of what he was already seeing, she thought, with a hollowing of her insides. Enjoying it a lot.

He didn't have sunglasses on, and his gaze was working over her slowly and deliberately. Though she was used to being looked at, it was usually for the sake of what she was wearing. Not for what she was *not* wearing...

Salvatore's lingering inspection was like a slow, burning flame licking over her body, heating it from the inside out, liquefying her...

Time seemed to stop, and her heart-rate began to thud within her, her blood quickening in her veins. Then, abruptly, he stopped looking. She could see it happen in his face, his eyes veiling. He resumed walking, raising a hand to her, but heading now for the pool house.

'I'm sorry for disturbing you,' he said casually, as he walked past her. 'I'm just going to change for a swim. You keep on sunbathing.'

Lana dropped her face again, still feeling the quickening of her blood. Willing it to subside. Conscious, with a silent gasp, that, even crushed as they were by her body weight on the lounger, her breasts had en-gorged, her nipples were cresting...

Oh, dear God—no! No, no and no!

She couldn't allow this. She mustn't! It was essential she didn't allow it! She buried her face in the towel and kept it resolutely there as she heard footsteps again, a heavy splash of pool water, then steady, rhythmic quieter splashing as Salvatore thrashed up and down the length of the pool. Eventually she heard him get out of the water, pat himself dry with a towel, and then bare feet approached her and a tall shadow fell over her.

'I really ought to put some after-sun cream on you,' he said, hunkering down beside her. 'Hold still.'

As he spoke, a dollop of cream, cold to her heated skin, was deposited between Lana's shoulder blades. A hand descended to anoint her.

'Relax,' Salvatore's deep voice admonished her.

It was an impossible command for Lana to obey—how could she possibly relax when the firm, smooth glide of his fingertips was working between her shoulder blades, down over the smooth expanse of her back? The cooling cream was soothing—but the stroke of his hands was the very opposite. A million nerve-endings fired simultaneously. She felt her hands claw into the towel, seeking self-control, willing herself not to react.

A moment later his hand was lifted from her, and he was straightening.

'All done,' he said. There was the slightest ragged edge to his voice. Then he was speaking again. 'I'll go and change in the pool house. You might want to turn over to protect your back.'

Now she fancied his voice was dry, not ragged. She heard him pad away, the pool house door open and shut. Instantly, her heart thudding hectically, she twisted her hands around her back to refasten the ties of her bikini top, then levered herself up to a sitting position, grabbing her wrap to tug it over her as quickly as she could. Before Salvatore emerged again.

When he did so, five minutes later, she was sitting up on the lounger, the back raised, demurely covered in the wrap, legs slanting sideways, dark glasses safely over her eyes, hair restrained by a ribboned tie. She was apparently absorbed in her paperback, reaching for her iced water. The image of cool, calm and collected.

A complete lie.

But one she had to hold to.

He paused by her lounger. 'Don't stay out too much longer,' he advised. 'There's still some heat in the sun.'

She gave an abstracted nod and he headed off. The moment he was gone she set down her book, swallowing hard. Staring helplessly out over the azure waters of the pool.

Heart still thudding.

Salvatore headed indoors. It had been sheer self-indulgence to put cream on her back as he had. But he didn't regret it. Why should he?

I know what I want of her.

Yes, he did indeed. And he would have a whole year of it. Unless, of course, he tired of her sooner. But that was for then. This was for now. And now was good.

He'd disposed of Giavanna, had been able to start the process of disposing with her father in his business affairs, and now he could focus on his other main purpose in bringing Lana out to Italy. Here, away from the non-stop social round in Rome, he could pursue his objective at his own pace.

It would have been preferable, obviously, simply to have been able to follow through on his initial intention to have an affair with her. Marrying her was a complication—but it was a necessary one. And now he'd achieved his purpose for marrying he could focus on Lana herself. The fact that she was his wife was to all intents and purposes irrelevant.

As he gained the landing his eyes went to the door of her bedroom, right next to his, just as it had been in Rome. And, as in the Rome apartment, her bedroom had once been his mother's and his, the master suite, his father's.

His expression changed. Became bleak for a moment.

Separated by a communicating door through which they did not communicate.

He pushed the bleak memory away, gained his own bedroom. He'd had it redecorated since his father's day, but it still brought a conflicting mix of affection and anger. His eyes went to the door that opened into Lana's room—his mother's bedroom. It felt odd to think of Lana there, making herself at home.

But she isn't—that's the point. She is merely passing through.

He dragged off his clothes, headed into the en suite bathroom. The vigorous swim had made him hungry for dinner. Putting cream on Lana's back had made him hungry to see her again.

Turning the dial to maximum force, he stepped inside the shower.

CHAPTER SIX

DINNER WAS SERVED in the elegant dining room, and although Salvatore had said the dress code was casual—something reflected both in her tunic-style rust-coloured dress with a dark scarf looped around her neck, and in Salvatore's fine cashmere sweater and dark trousers—simply sitting there at the polished mahogany table, surrounded by landscape paintings that Lana was pretty sure might equally be hanging in a museum, and being waited on by the two man-servants overseen by the stately Giuseppe, was hardly, she thought, a casual experience. Nor was the meal itself, which consisted of the full panoply of courses—from an *aperitivo* served by Giuseppe himself, all the way through to the *dolce*, which was a delicate pear *sorbetto*.

'This is in your honour,' Salvatore murmured to her *sotto voce*.

Dutifully, Lana voiced her thanks, and determined to be vocally appreciative of every offering—which was not in the least hard to do, for everything served was delicious and she ate with gusto. She felt she was winning Giuseppe's approval, and felt a pang of guilt. He was treating her as the new mistress of the *palazzo*, when she was no such thing.

Nor will I ever be.

Her gaze went to Salvatore, sitting at the head of the table. Because of the table's length, she was not sitting at the foot but at his right-hand side, less than a metre from him, as if they really were a married couple. Something that was not an ache—it *couldn't* be an ache…there was no reason for it to be an ache, and certainly no justification—formed inside her.

Then he was speaking again, and the ache was dispelled. Discarded. It had no place, anyway.

She paid attention to what he was saying. He was no longer using the brisk, impersonal, imperious manner that he had during their first few days in Rome when had had been speaking to her alone, giving her instructions. He was more relaxed here—that much was obvious. Unless, of course, she realised belatedly, that that was simply for the benefit of his household.

For herself, though, she was not relaxed. She'd tried to hide it—again for the benefit of the household. But the incident by the pool still disturbed her. She must make sure, she resolved, that nothing like that could ever happen again.

'So, would you like to see Florence tomorrow?' Salvatore enquired.

'Tomorrow?' Lana echoed, slightly surprised. After all, he was under no obligation to entertain her.

'It would suit me,' he replied. 'The following day I have conference calls morning and afternoon.'

'Then, thank you, yes, I would love to see Florence,' Lana dutifully agreed.

The remainder of the meal was spent discussing their itinerary for Florence. Lana readily agreed to forego the Uffizi this time around, to focus on a more general tour of the city's main highlights.

'There will be plenty of opportunity for you to visit as often as you wish,' Salvatore said.

She nodded in polite agreement. She was already thinking ahead to when she would be left to her own devices. She would use the opportunity of living in Italy for the duration of her marriage to learn the language. She would learn off the Internet...buy textbooks. It would be something to take away from her time here...

Her gaze flickered to Salvatore again.

She felt again, just for a fraction of a moment, that irrelevant tiny ache which had neither cause, nor justification, nor any business at all being there. So what if he was the most lethal-looking man she'd ever seen in her life? So what if he had eyed her up while she was sunbathing and put cream on her back? None of that had any place in the reason why she had married him.

That was all she had to remember.

Florence was everything its reputation said it would be and more. Lana was entranced, despite the crowds even this early in the season, and gazing about her avidly. Salvatore made an expert guide, his long familiarity with the city enabling her to make sense of all that she was seeing.

She'd worn a comfortable outfit quite deliberately—a crisply cut sand-coloured shirt dress and a loose jacket, which looked both casual and chic worn with day-proof flats that would cope with a lot of walking. Which they did.

They took in all the main sights, starting with Michelangelo's *David* and the basilica, and going on from there. Lana's head was reeling from all the information Salvatore was giving her, amplified by guidebooks and Internet. The weather was ideal—not too hot, and very pleasant. Even so, she was glad to stop for lunch, to be taken outdoors at an upmarket trattoria. Lana, still celebrating the end of her modelling diet, focussed on pasta—Salvatore on veal escalope.

Then they forayed forth again to cross the River Arno by the famous covered Ponte Vecchio bridge, where Salvatore regaled her with the tale of how the Medicis had had a secret crossing constructed within the bridge as a potential escape route from their city rivals, and how the disastrous floods a generation earlier had caused appalling damage to the city, from which it had now, thankfully, recovered.

Another break for coffee ensued, and then, as the afternoon sun lengthened, they ascended to the Piazzale Michelangelo above the city—the terrace that gave sweeping picture-postcard views over the whole panorama.

'Time for cocktails,' Salvatore announced, when Lana had had her fill of gazing. 'Then dinner. We're booked at the rooftop restaurant at the Falcone—you'll like it.'

Lana looked at him a little uncertainly. He'd spent the day showing her Florence—did he really want to dine out with her there as well?

'You don't have to,' she said. 'You've given up an entire day to me as it is.'

Salvatore's expression was unreadable. It was strange for her to see it like that again, for during the day he'd been more relaxed—more affable—than she had yet experienced. Perhaps, she thought, it was because there were no eyes on him…neither his staff's, nor his friends', nor his social acquaintances'.

We're anonymous here—I don't have to role-play, and neither does he. He's just a native Italian, showing Firenze off to an English tourist.

But now, somehow, that had gone.

'It's all arranged,' he said, as if brooking no contestation of what he wanted.

'Then of course…' Lana said acquiescently.

She wasn't dressed for somewhere as swanky as the Falcone was obviously going to be, but if that didn't bother Salvatore it need not bother her. He was casually dressed himself, in an open-neck shirt and linen jacket, with light trousers and, like her, comfortable walking shoes. She gave an inward sigh. He looked as drop-dead gorgeous in this outfit as he did in every other. Wearing dark glasses, as he had for much of the day, only added to it.

What am I going to do about this…?

The troubling thought plucked at her. She needed to stop being so aware of him physically the whole time. She had a whole year to get through, after all.

Perhaps, after a few weeks—a few months—the constant awareness would wear off.

It was a frail hope, but the only one available.

Salvatore sat back in his chair at their table on the roof terrace of the Falcone and looked across at the woman he was dining with. She looked as effortlessly beautiful as ever. Her dress might be casual, her hair drawn back in a plait that she'd wound around itself at the nape of her neck to keep it out of the way and her make-up nothing more than mascara and lip gloss. But that did not detract from her allure one iota.

She possessed a naturally bestowed beauty that had had male heads turning all day. She'd seemed oblivious to it—or perhaps, given her career, simply indifferent. He was glad of it. There was only one man he didn't want her indifferent to.

Except… His face tightened minutely. That seemed to be exactly what she was to him. Even after spending a day with her he saw nothing in her behaviour that had not been there before. She'd shown interest in what he was telling her, asked pertinent questions, displayed an informed level of general knowledge about the Renaissance. But nothing more than that.

She was civil and polite, but…

Guarded. Was that the word for the way she was with him?

Perhaps, though, he only had himself to blame for that. His state of tension when he'd first arrived in Rome had made him, he acknowledged, less than relaxed with her. He'd needed her to get it all right, what he required of her, to perform the way he'd wanted her to do.

Now, though, with mission accomplished—Giavanna stymied and her father perforce accepting his ambitions had been thwarted—away from the fishbowl and gossip hive of Rome, he could afford to be more relaxed.

And so could she.

He'd chosen the rooftop restaurant of the Falcone hotel for its famous vista over the rooftops of Florence, looking towards the basilica. The evening was warm, the lights low, and the candles on the tables were throwing a soft glow over the scene. It had been a long day, and both of them had been glad to sit down and make their choices from the superb menu. Now, as they sipped their *aperitivos*, Salvatore's eyes went to Lana, who was gazing appreciatively out over the city. For himself, he was gazing appreciatively over *her*.

'So, have you enjoyed today?' he asked.

She turned back at his question, a smile on her face. 'Yes, indeed. How could I not? It's been very good of you.'

He made a negating gesture with his hand. 'I was happy to do so,' he said.

There was a hint of brusqueness in his voice—impatience, even, and he was aware of it. Aware of why it was there. She didn't have to tell him it had been 'good' of him, as if he were doing her a favour he did not need to. Or want to.

'Next time,' he went on, 'you shall see the Uffizi. A private tour would be best.'

She shook her head. 'Oh, no, please don't. That's quite unnecessary. A timed booking to avoid the queues would be fine, and much less expensive.'

He raised an eyebrow. She came from a different world from him. It had been easy to forget that this last week, showing her off in Rome, couture-gowned and wearing jewellery she'd never be able to afford in all her life.

And now she is my wife.

Except that had it not been for the necessity of spiking Roberto's guns she would not be his wife at all. She'd be here as his latest *inamorata*—nothing more than that. He found his gaze slipping down to where her wedding band glinted in the candlelight as she lifted her glass to her lips. His own glinted too.

He drew a breath, not wanting to think about it. Marriage had been necessary—that was all there was to it. It was irrelevant, therefore, that it had not been by choice.

When would it ever be by choice?

The caustic words shaped in his head, long familiar to him.

'A private tour is far preferable,' he said, closing the subject. 'I'll arrange it for next time we come here.'

The waiter was hovering to take their order, and he turned his attention to that instead. The cuisine at the Falcone was first class, and never disappointed.

Nor did it tonight and nor did the company. Or the ambience. As the meal progressed he made a focussed effort to set Lana at her ease. To put aside the tensions that had inevitably surrounded their time in

Rome, where it had been essential she play her part to perfection.

Here, now, it was different.

Not having to act—play the bride and groom to everyone. Just being ourselves instead...

Relaxing after an enjoyable day. Setting aside any consciousness of the fact that they were married, because here, and now, it was completely irrelevant. Because here and now, as dusk faded and night gathered, the city lights pricking out beneath the unseen stars, only one thing mattered. Just as it had from the very first.

The fact that he desired her.

And the fact that she was also, as it happened, his wife, for the purposes for which he'd married her and for no other reason at all, was of no account at all.

There was wedding her and there was bedding her—and they were completely separate.

Lana drained the last of her wine, setting the glass back on the damask linen tablecloth. Her mood was strange. She had spoken the truth when she'd told Salvatore she'd enjoyed the day—how could anyone possibly not enjoy a day in Florence?

And with him to show it to me.

Her eyes went to him now, as he sat relaxed back in his chair, looking as lethal as ever. Somehow even more so, she thought, lounged back as he was, his wine glass held between long fingers, the open collar of his shirt framing the strong column of his neck, dark glasses casually pushed back on his sable hair. At his jaw the

very faintest shadowing was visible, giving him a raff-
ish allure. An allure of which two glasses of wine and
an *aperitivo* was making her more than ever aware.

She was also all too conscious that it was enhanced
by where they were—dining up here amongst the rooftops of Florence, beneath the stars. So ridiculously romantic...

Except that she must not think of it that way.

No, they were simply having dinner together, and
the fact that they happened to be in such a ridiculously
romantic location was nothing to do with them. Salvatore had chosen the spot because of the view and
the excellence of the food. Their conversation over
the meal had been innocuous, nothing personal—only
about what they'd seen and what there was yet to see,
both in Florence and in Tuscany further afield. It could
have been a conversation between any two people, not
herself and Salvatore. Not between two newlyweds.

*But the marriage is irrelevant. It has nothing to do
with us as people. It isn't real at a personal level—
how could it be?*

There was nothing personal between them at all.

She dragged her gaze away from him, back over
the rooftops of Florence. A much safer view than gazing at Salvatore.

She realised Salvatore was speaking again, diverting
her thoughts from where it was pointless for them to go.

'Do you know the story of how the architect
Brunelleschi won the competition for constructing
what was then the biggest dome in the world for the
basilica?'

She frowned slightly, looking across at him as she answered. 'My father explained it to me once—something about there being two domes, one inside the other, and the smaller one helped support the larger one?' she ventured.

'*Essatamente,*' said Salvatore.

'My father always wanted to come and see it for himself. He and my mother were planning a holiday here when—' She broke off, giving a slight shrug. 'Well, they never made it here.' Her voice was flat.

Her gaze went out over the rooftops again, towards the floodlit basilica with its famed octagonal *cupula.* Her throat had tightened. Painful emotion bit as she thought of her parents and their untimely deaths.

Then suddenly she felt her hand, lying on the tabletop, being pressed lightly.

Sympathetically.

'Then they'll be glad, won't they, your parents, that you are here to see it for them?' Salvatore said quietly.

Lana turned her head back. The look on his face was one of understanding, and she felt herself blink unaccountably. Then it was his gaze that was looking away. Far away...

'My mother always loved Firenze,' he said slowly, automatically giving the Italian name for Florence, Lana realised. 'It gave her so much inspiration for the *palazzo.* She loved to browse here in all the antiques shops, buying furniture and art. It kept her occupied when—'

He broke off, made a slightly apologetic face at Lana. 'I'm sorry. Ancient history.' He reached for the wine bottle, pouring a little into Lana's glass and into his, finishing the bottle.

'Please don't apologise,' Lana said, her voice low and full of emotion. 'Our memories are all we have and we must treasure them.'

She had heard the affection in his voice as he'd spoken of his mother, and knew without him telling her that she had been loved by him. She felt emotion come again—but this time for him, not for herself. Because he, like she, had suffered so grievous a loss.

He looked across at her. Was it the candlelight, or the wine, or the stars still dim in the sky above? Whatever it was there was something in his face, in his eyes, that had not been there before. Something in his gaze.

'You are right—we must,' he said. 'For their sakes as well as ours. The good memories—yes, those we must remember and cherish.'

He held her gaze. Then, lifting his wine glass, he titled it at her. The ruby wine caught the candle flame, reflected it in its depths. It was reflected in the depths of his dark eyes too, lightening them.

'And this will be one of them,' he said. His voice was different now. Lighter, like the expression in his eyes. 'So let's drink to it.'

She reached for her glass, not dropping his gaze, letting him touch her glass with his.

'*Saluti,*' he said. 'To a good day, a relaxing gourmet evening—and to all that is yet to come.'

For a moment—just a moment—she felt something flicker deep inside her, as if the flame reflected in the

wine and in his dark eyes were flickering inside her
as well.

Then he was taking a mouthful of the wine, draining
his glass. He lifted a hand, summoned a waiter to their
table with an easy gesture, asked for the dessert menu.

'The *dulce* here are famed!' he told Lana smil-
ingly. 'And since you are off your model's diet you
can indulge to the max. Indulge,' he said, and his long
lashes swept momentarily down over his eyes, 'in everything...'

Was there a husk in his voice? She was imagining it,
surely. There was no need for her to hear one. No need
for anything, in fact, except to take the gilt-edged menu
card being presented to her by the returning waiter and
put her mind to the tempting task of selecting something highly calorific and even more delicious.

The *dulce*, after all, were all that she must be
tempted by.

Dulce... she thought driftingly, as she made her
choice—a rich, caramel-based *crema* that Salvatore
had recommended as a speciality of the house and
which she had been happy to agree to—*dulce* meant
'sweet'. Her gaze went back to Salvatore as he relayed
their identical choice to the waiter, who disappeared
off.

*And this is sweet—this whole evening with him.
Sweet to sit here, high over this fabled city, wining
and dining, just us, together, not on show, not pretending to be what we are not—just being who we are.*

The wine was sweet in her veins, the air sweet in
her throat, and the sight of Salvatore, so incredibly

good-looking, so impossible to tear her gaze from, so sweet to gaze at...

She knew she was a little intoxicated—knew it and didn't mind...didn't care. Knew that it was good—*sweet*—just to sit here, in this beautiful place, with the ambience, the view, the warmth all around her and Salvatore to gaze at...

He met her gaze. Smiled.

And it seemed very good to her.

Sweet.

I don't want this to end. The thought moved through her head. *I want to go on sitting here, gazing at him, because it's all I want to do.*

It was strange... Strange because a stranger was what he was to her. What else could he be?

It was a question she should not have asked. Because it came with an answer that was impossible. Just impossible.

He is no longer a stranger to me.

The lights of the *palazzo* were welcoming in the velvet night as Salvatore got out of the car, turning back to help Lana out. She did not take his outstretched hand, merely stepped out with the natural elegance with which she always carried herself. Salvatore closed her door and nodded goodnight to his chauffeur. The car crunched slowly away around to the garages at the rear. As it departed Salvatore glanced at Lana, ready to usher her indoors, but she was standing gazing upwards.

'What a glorious starry night!' she exclaimed. 'We

couldn't see it nearly as well in Florence, with the city lights.'

Salvatore followed her gaze. It was, indeed, a glorious starry night, with the Milky Way sweeping over the *palazzo*. Then his eyes dropped to Lana. Her uplifted face, the long, graceful line of her exposed throat and the soft contour of the plaited coil of her hair at the nape of her neck were all dimly lit by starlight and the few lights showing inside the *palazzo*, giving her an ethereal quality.

Instinct took over. Impulse. He stepped towards her.

All evening his consciousness of her had been growing and growing. To sit with her on the Falcone's rooftop terrace, bathed in soft light, catching her fragrance in the warmth of the evening as the light dimmed and the city took on the glow of the night, its monuments bathed in iridescent up-lights… With no one but themselves to pay attention to, for all the other diners had only had eyes for each other in that most romantic of locales.

And I had eyes only for her—for her exquisite beauty.

And there had been something else too, he knew. Something that had come as they had touched upon the strange circumstances of their lives that were shared, each of them having lost their parents to tragic accident.

He felt emotion—alien, but present—move in him. Desire, yes, but something else, too. Something that had started to form, to flow between them. Something he was not used to.

Something that seemed to intensity her beauty…

His eyes shaped her uplifted face… He said her name. Wanting her to look not at the starlit sky, but at him. 'Lana…'

His voice was husky. Sitting beside her in the back seat on the journey home, with the wine from their meal warming his veins, the scent of her faint perfume had caught at him. Knowing she was only a hand's reach away from him in the dark interior of the car as it had hummed along the autostrada had been a torment.

They'd hardly spoken on the journey, only to make inconsequential remarks about the events of the day, but Salvatore had been endlessly aware of her presence so close to him, so private, with the glass screen dividing them from his driver, who'd been focussing on the road ahead. He'd allowed himself the luxury of glancing at her from time to time, after conversation had ceased, and had seen that she had closed her eyes, as if in sleep. But he was pretty sure she had not been sleeping. One hand had rested on the door, and by its position he'd been able to tell that her muscles had not been relaxed. Nor had her breathing been that of someone dozing.

The thought had occurred to him that she was deliberately feigning sleep in order to withdraw from him. He did not want her withdrawing from him. Did not want her gazing up at the stars now.

The wine he'd drunk at dinner was accentuating his senses, his awareness of her.

His desire for her.

It rose in his veins, sweet and rich.

From the very first he had held back, knowing he must focus on the business of his marriage, on the reason he had undertaken it, on facing outward to the world.

But there was no more need for that. Now he could give free rein to what he had felt from the very first moment of setting eyes on her. No more delays, no more holding back. For either of them.

That kiss he'd taken from her the very first night he'd taken her out to show all of Rome his new bride had told him what awaited him. That she would return all he wanted of her.

She desires me, even as I desire her.

And now—oh, now that desire between them could blossom and flourish and be fulfilled.

As he said her name, his voice husky, she lowered her gaze from the star-filled sky to meet his. For a second—an instant, a timeless moment—he held her eyes with his. Then his hand reached out, folded around her upper arm as he stepped towards her, closing the distance between them. He said her name again, and his other hand—of its own volition, it seemed—cupped her cheek. She stood completely motionless, but there was something in her gaze as he poured his eyes into hers that seemed captive…helpless.

Wordlessly, he bent his head to hers, let his mouth do what it ached to do again—to feel the velvet touch of her lips beneath his, to softly press itself to hers. He heard the low, soft sigh in her throat as her lips parted for his, her body inclined towards his. His hand around her arm tightened automatically to support her pliant body…so pliant, and the fingers at her cheek speared into her golden hair, holding her for his deepening kiss.

Blood surged in his veins, desire flaring strong and insistent. This—*this* was what he had wanted, ached for, ever since he had first seen her…ever since that first tantalising kiss he'd drawn from her that night at the Duchessa's. He drew her against him, his kiss deepening, letting go her arm to fasten his arm around her slender waist, holding her for his desire and his sweet, sweet pleasure.

And for hers.

He felt it—felt her respond to him, felt her mouth open to his, her kiss deepen even as his did. Felt her hands lift to his chest, splaying out across it, and low in her throat he heard, with triumphant exultation, a low, helpless moan. Desire surged more strongly yet, released from the thrall he had imposed upon it—had had to impose upon it. But now, gloriously, triumphantly, he could let it loose upon her, let it loose within him.

He gave himself to it—to the arousal mounting within him, the arousal he could sense with every long-honed masculine instinct was possessing her too, binding her to him, and he to her. Their bodies pressed against each other, her breasts peaking against the hard wall of his chest. He wanted more—and yet more…

And then, like a douche of cold water, she wrenched herself free, jolting back. Stepping away.

'*No!*'

A single word. A single forbidding edict. A single denial.

He stared at her, disbelieving, while the blood

pounded in his head, scythed through his veins. He saw her hold up her hands, palms out, as if to ward him off. Her eyes were wide, distended.

'No!' she said again, and took a further step back. 'It's impossible—' Her voice seemed to shake, and she took a shuddering breath, hands still held up. 'We *can't*,' she said, her gaze still stricken.

He stared at her. *'Can't?'* he echoed blankly. The word made no sense.

But she said it again. 'We *can't*,' she repeated, as vehemently as the first time.

Her hands were still warding him off. She was backing away from him now—backing towards the front door as if trying to seek refuge from him by going indoors. He was still wordless with shock and incomprehension. And with a frustration that was biting through him in disbelief.

She was speaking again, throwing words at him. 'Look, we've both drunk too much wine...spent too long alone together. We're acting under impulse. Because of the wine, the night, the stars, whatever—' She broke off, dropping her hands in a defeated gesture.

He was still standing there immobile, frozen. Uncomprehending.

'Why?' he heard himself say. 'Why are you saying *can't*? Do you think I don't know when a woman is responsive? You flamed in my arms just now—'

Her voice cut across his, urgent and denying. 'Of *course* I'm saying *can't*! How could it possibly be anything else! How could you *think* it could be anything else?'

He saw her shut her eyes for a moment, draw a ragged breath. Then her eyes flew open again, and her words were vehement and stabbing.

'How,' she said, her voice ragged, 'can it possibly be anything other than *can't* when you are *paying* me to be here with you?'

If he'd frozen before, he did so again now—totally.

'*Paying* you?' There was Arctic ice in Salvatore's voice.

He saw her face work in the dim starlight. Her hands raised again to ward him off. Heard the consternation in her face, her voice.

'What else do you call it? Salvatore, I'm only here— only with you at all—because you are paying me *four hundred thousand pounds* to be here!'

A hand slashed down through the air. He realised it was his own.

'*Como?* You say that to me? You say such a thing?' A furious breath was exhaled from him. His eyes flashed with outrage at the words she had thrown at him. 'That money,' he bit out, 'is the sum agreed in the prenup you signed. It is a divorce settlement. It is *not*,' he ground out, black fury in him, 'a *payment* to you for your presence here!'

He could see her face working again, her hands dropping heavily to her sides, as heavy as her voice.

'Of course it is! What else can it be? It's the reason I married you—so you would pay off my mortgage for me! It's *money* that brought me here, Salvatore! I'm your employee, or as good as! Nothing more than that. You know our marriage is a lie as much as I do! It's a fiction, however legal it may be! And it doesn't matter whether you call that four hundred thousand pounds I'm going to get when you dispose of that fiction a divorce settlement or a pay-out—it's *payment* for my being here, for going through that marriage ceremony with you! So if I…if you…if…'

She lifted her hands again, stepping another pace backwards.

'If there is *anything* else between us other than what we've established so far…a…a working relationship, if you want to call it that, then what that amounts to… what that makes me…is—'

She broke off. Looked straight at him, let her hands drop again. Her voice changed. Became painful. Halting. It hurt him to hear it. Appalled him.

'I'm spending a year of my life with you, Salvatore, in the role of your wife. The *public* role of your wife. Not personal—*never* personal. It can't be. *Nothing* can be personal between us! Not beyond the remit of a working relationship! At the end of the year I walk away with four hundred thousand pounds. That's it, Salvatore—nothing more. So it can't…*can't* be anything more. It just *can't*.'

She shook her head, backing further away from him.

'I'm… I'm sorry—'

Her voice broke and he saw her swallow painfully, chokingly.

'Sorry that I let you kiss me. I apologise if it…gave you ideas. Ideas that can't exist for the reasons I've given. I won't go down that path. I can't. I can't separate the money I'm being paid for marrying you from what you…what you want of me. Even…' she swallowed again, more painfully yet '… even if it's what I gave you the impression of wanting. The two don't go together. They can't. I'm sorry if you don't see it that way—but I do.'

She turned away, walking indoors. He watched her go.

Ice in his veins.

But something quite different in his guts.

CHAPTER SEVEN

LANA STOOD BENEATH the pounding shower, water sluicing over her. She wished it would wash away her tor-
mented thoughts, rinse the heated blood from her body.
But it did no such thing. When she emerged, wrapped
in a fleecy towel, she felt no less agitated than when
she'd fled from him.

From Salvatore.

From the man who was her husband—in name only.

Because it has to be that way—and stay that way!

That was essential. Imperative. Because otherwise...

Memory, hot and humid, flared within her. In an
instant she was back outside, hearing Salvatore say
her name, hearing the desire in it, feeling her own response to it flare, standing there, quite motionless, with
only the sudden thudding of her heart in anticipation...

*If only I hadn't got out of the car and stared up at
the stars as I did! If I'd just gone straight indoors! Said
goodnight and thank you and headed straight upstairs!
I could have... I could have—*

Could have maintained the front she'd managed to

preserve all evening, dining at that ridiculously romantic rooftop restaurant, letting that vintage wine seep
into her veins, doing its disastrous work, lowering the
defences she had erected from the very first moment
she'd ever set eyes on Salvatore! Had had to erect.

Because anything else—

*Is impossible—just impossible! Impossible because
it's just so complicated! Being here, being his legal wife
but not his real wife! Knowing I only married him to get
my pay-off at the end. So I can't... I just can't...make
things ever more complicated between us—*

Her own desperate words to him out there under the
stars burned in her head again, as her eyes went now
to the door between their bedrooms.

Closed.

The way it had to be.

Salvatore stared at the screen in his office in the *palazzo*, but he wasn't taking in what was on it. He'd slept
badly—restlessly—frustratedly. And he was frustrated
not just physically, from being denied what his body
had so blatantly told him it wanted. No, it was more
than just physical.

Lana's outburst had shocked him—stopped him in
his tracks, quite literally. He still could not believe what
she had thrown at him.

*How can she possibly think that I would take any
notice whatsoever of the financial aspect of our divorce
agreement at such a moment? And how could she think
about it either? Neither the reason we married, nor the
outcome of our eventual divorce, has anything to do*

with what there is between us—what has been there from the very first!

Somehow he had to make her see that. Had to make her see that the reason they had married was irrelevant to what had drawn him to her that very first evening… what had been in her lips when he had kissed her…

He drew a breath, reaching for his keyboard. He had a video conference to join. Work would distract him. And right now distraction was what he needed.

Tonight… Yes, tonight he would start to win Lana back after he had so disastrously scared her off. He did not want to make a mess of it a second time.

For a tantalising moment her image floated in his mind. How lovely she was—and how much he desired her! But his desire for her was not enough—*she* must accept hers for him. Accept that what drew them to each other was nothing to do with the artifice of their marriage.

It's between us personally—between her and me.

And that was the way he wanted it to be. Nothing to do with their marriage.

Because marriage—real, lasting marriage, to any woman—was not something he ever wanted to have anything to do with.

Cautiously, Lana made her way out on to the dining terrace. The warmth of the evening was balmy, but it was at odds with the tension inside her that had been there all day, even though she'd thankfully not set eyes on Salvatore at all.

Now, walking out on to the stone terrace in the

balmy evening, she saw that he was already there, looking towards her. A bottle of champagne was in a cooler by the table which was set for dinner, soft candles already lit in their glass holders. She glanced warily at the open champagne bottle, smoking gently. What was going on?

Please, please don't let this be some kind of seduction scene! Not after the disaster of last night!

Her eyes went to Salvatore, her expression still wary. He was looking as gorgeous as ever, a loose-knit cotton sweater in moss-green and a pair of well-cut chinos emphasising his lean, fit build and declaring his innate Italian sense of style, but there was a look on his face that she'd not seen before. Apologetic.

He gave her a brief constrained smile. 'I'm sorry,' he said, 'about last night.'

Lana swallowed, her mouth dry suddenly.

'I don't want you stressing about it,' Salvatore went on. He was holding her gaze, his expression intent. 'I want you to be comfortable here—comfortable with me.'

He took a step towards her. His expression changed suddenly. Softened. Gently, with one finger, he touched her cheek—a fleeting moment only—looking down at her out of deep, long-lashed eyes, their darkness unfathomable.

'So—are we all right together?'

She swallowed again, feeling the trace of his fleeting touch on her cheek. Then she made herself nod.

He smiled. A warm, genuine smile. '*Bene*—I am glad.' Then he moved towards the champagne cooler, lifted the bottle from it. Looked back at her. 'Let's drink to that,' he said.

His voice was lighter now, she could hear it, and she could see it in his expression too. She felt something lighten in herself as well. She watched him fill two slanted flutes in turn, judging the effervescence with practised skill, then he replaced the bottle and picked up the frothing glasses, handing one to her. She took it gingerly, not wanting their fingers to touch for reasons she didn't want to think about—for the reasons he'd just kicked into touch by what he'd said to her.

He lifted his glass, tilting it slightly towards her. 'To being comfortable with each other,' he said. There was a wry smile in his voice, on his lips, in his dark, unfathomable eyes.

She didn't reply, not sure what to say, but lifted her glass, let him clink his lightly against hers, then took a mouthful as he did from his. The mousse was chill, cooling the heat that had suddenly flushed her face—mistakenly, surely?

He set down his glass, smiled at her. A reassuring smile. 'And now, with our new understanding, we shall enjoy an excellent dinner!' he announced.

As if on cue, as they sat down at the table, one of the two manservants appeared, placing a bowl of plump olives on the table and a plate of crostini canapés. Salvatore exchanged pleasantries with the young man, who responded in kind.

He's polite to his staff...courteous and considerate, Lana could not but observe. Did that include herself?

After all, she'd said last night that she was really nothing more than a kind of employee.

But even as she'd called herself that she had known it was not true. It was far more complicated than that. No employee would sit here like this, sipping champagne with him, dining with him, just the two of them…

She reached for an olive, plump and glistening with rich oil, taking a delicate bite from it to stop herself thinking about what it was, exactly, that she and Salvatore were to each other.

'What do you make of them?' Salvatore was asking, helping himself to one of the large, luscious olives as well. 'They're from the estate here.'

Lana swallowed the rest of her olive. 'Oh, I didn't realise there was land attached to the *palazzo* other than the gardens.'

'Oh, yes, there's an extensive estate—olive groves, farmland, vineyards, woodlands… The wine is nothing spectacular, but I'm reserving an interest in wine-making for my old age! I'll do something about improving it then,' Salvatore replied lightly.

He started to tell her about the traditional grapes of the region, and Lana listened with half an ear, knowing little about wine but grateful that it was an innocuous subject. As she sipped at her champagne, nibbling the delicious olives and the equally delicious crostini, salty with anchovy and goat's cheese, she started—thankfully—to feel the tension that had racked her all day—and all the previous night—begin to ease from her.

Comfortable—that was what Salvatore had said he

wanted them to be together. *And maybe we can be. However complicated the situation between us is—*

Her eyes rested on him momentarily as he waxed lyrical about Tuscan grape varieties. She felt her breath catch. He really was just so gorgeous...

She fought to clamp down on her reaction. What had happened last night had been a mistake—that was all. An impulse neither of them should have succumbed to. And now he'd apologised for it and put it aside.

So I don't have to think about it any more. Or feel awkward about it. Or feel awkward around him.

She made herself focus on what he was telling her, asking him a question she hoped wasn't too distracted. The young manservant appeared again, bearing a tray of more dishes, one of which he reverently placed on the table. Salvatore said something appreciative in Italian, and then turned to Lana.

'Black truffles,' he announced as the manservant took his leave. 'From our very own woods—but if I told you exactly where I'd have to shoot you!'

It was humorously said, and Lana gave the expected laugh, glad to do so. Glad to sip at her champagne, too, letting it help her set aside any obsessing about the complications of why she was here with Salvatore in the first place, the confusing tensions those complications engendered whenever she gazed at him in all his gorgeousness. She felt herself start to relax little by little, glad just to listen to him descant on the art of truffle-hunting, on the incredible noses of the trained dogs that sniffed out the prized treasures from under the earth and leaf mould.

As he did so, he shaved two of them into razor-thin slices, proffering them to her. 'Try them neat, before they go on the risotto,' he recommended.

She took a tiny sliver, tasting it somewhat tentatively. 'Oh, that is good!' she exclaimed.

'Isn't it?' he agreed, and then proceeded to scatter generous amounts on their respective servings of risotto.

With a will, Lana tucked in. The rich creaminess of the risotto was brilliantly offset by the musky earthiness of the truffle, and she ate with her eyes half shut to get the full impact. With a sigh, she set her fork aside, her dish empty.

'We'll save some truffle for the *secondo*,' Salvatore announced. 'It's going to be venison.'

It was—and, again, the combination of the strong-tasting meat and the distinctive truffle worked superbly, and the wine that was served alongside it was strong enough to withstand the robust flavours.

'Sangiovese grapes,' Salvatore informed her, lifting his glass to her. *'Saluti!'*

She murmured in reply. She was feeling easier now, she knew, and was glad of it.

We're just enjoying the moment, the delicious food, this beautiful place...just enjoying each other's company. Knowing—and accepting, both of us—that there can be nothing more between us.

Did a quiver of regret go through her? Her eyes lingered on him for a moment as the dusk gathered, as it had last night in that ridiculously romantic rooftop

restaurant in Florence, drinking in the way it accentuated the planes of his face.

She suppressed a sigh, returning to her meal. Wanting no more complications.

Across the table, Salvatore watched her eat with lidded
eyes. He had caught the half-suppressed sigh…caught
the covert glance she'd given him. But he let them be.
He was doing what he knew he must do now—focussing only on undoing the damage he'd inadvertently
done last night, rushing her as he had.

His eyes moved over her. She was casually dressed
in black leggings, with a loose, thigh-length charcoal-
grey top. Elegant, but figure-concealing. Deliberately
so, he surmised. Wariness had radiated from her on all
frequencies as she'd emerged onto the terrace, and he'd
known immediately that he must disarm it. The fact
that he had succeeded was evident. Over the course of
the meal she had visibly relaxed, and he was glad of it.

But there was a way to go yet before she yielded to
what he longed for and forgot all about the artifice of
their marriage.

Made the reason that they were together simply…
personal.

'Ready for the off?' Salvatore's tone was genial as
Lana came down the grand staircase, attired for another day's sightseeing.

It had become the norm over the last week or more
for Salvatore to intersperse the days he spent incar-

cerated in his high-tech office, commanding his business affairs, with expeditions designed to show Lana the glories of Tuscany. As well as Florence, she could now add Pisa, Lucca and Sienna to her collection. Today's expedition was to be further afield, so Salvatore had told her. They'd be heading up into the higher hills, a more remote part of Tuscany, off the standard tourist trail.

He'd made no attempt to be anything other than good, easy-going company, and Lana found she was being the same in return. What they talked about she was never quite sure, in retrospect. About the places he was showing her, yes, and ordinary chit-chat, but precisely about what was vague. Maybe that was a good sign, though, she thought. A sign of how comfortable they had become with each other. Almost unconsciously so, now she thought about it.

It's done us good, she thought, greeting him airily as they made their way outside on to the *palazzo*'s gravelled carriage sweep.

Only as she felt the morning's heat envelop her did she feel a flickering thought fleeting across her mind.

Us? Is that what there is now? An 'us'?

But then it had gone.

Her eyes went to the rugged-looking SUV parked up for them—a far cry from either Salvatore's low-slung supercar or the sleek saloon they used when they were being chauffeured.

'Better for the steeper terrain,' he said, helping her up into the front passenger seat before vaulting in on his side and gunning the engine.

And so it proved as they reached what she thought was their destination—a walled hilltop town with vertiginous drops to the steep-sided valley below. But she discovered they were only stopping there for an early lunch, which they had at a quaint old trattoria in the small central *piazza*, while Salvatore told them of his plans for the afternoon.

'There's a lake nearby—higher up—that was formed by damming the river, with forest all around. It's very beautiful and I thought it would make a change for us,' he told her. 'A touch of "wild Italy", so to speak.' He smiled.

The lakeside was reached by a winding, unmetalled roadway which ended beneath a canopy of trees. They got out, and Lana was glad that Salvatore had advised sturdy shoes as well as comfortable leggings and a light sweatshirt. After a short walk through the thick trees, they emerged beside the water. A few metres back from the shore was a small chalet in log cabin style, with a shaded veranda at the front.

'Oh, how picturesque!' she exclaimed when she saw it.

Salvatore turned to her, a half smile on his face. 'Do you like it?' he asked.

'Perfect for the spot!' Lana confirmed with an answering smile.

He nodded. 'Good. It's where we're staying.'

CHAPTER EIGHT

'*Staying?*'

Salvatore could hear the bewilderment in Lana's voice and hoped he'd made the right call. He wanted Lana entirely to himself, without anyone else around— not even the staff at the *palazzo*—and if she agreed to it this remote chalet, hired for the week, was ideal for that. Here, they could completely forget that they'd gone through a marriage ceremony that had absolutely no relevance to why they were together in this secluded hideaway.

'Come and see what you make of it,' he invited.

Lightly vaulting up the veranda steps, he opened the door. Inside it was rustically simple—a single room with a long, comfortable-looking settee, some woven rugs on the floor, a small dining table with two wooden chairs, and a log-burner stove set into a thick stone chimney breast. At the rear a kitchenette was tucked beneath what was little more than a ladder leading up to a narrow mezzanine beneath the rafters, the entire space of which was taken up by a bed.

He stepped back.

Lana, with a wary expression on her face, looked in, her gaze sweeping up to the mezzanine. Then she looked back at Salvatore. 'And where,' she asked, her voice deliberate, 'is the other bedroom?'

He was unfazed. 'The settee is long enough to sleep on—plus there's a camp bed that can be placed on the veranda. It's quite warm enough for me to sleep out, so don't worry about that.'

The look she threw at him was old-fashioned in the extreme.

He touched her wrist lightly. Made his voice encouraging. 'Lana, we've been on show ever since we tied the knot—first in Rome and then, yes, even at the *palazzo*, playing "the bride and groom" even if only for the staff. Even sightseeing there have been people everywhere! Here we can just—what's that English word?—chillax. Be ourselves...not what others think we are. Doesn't that appeal?'

He gestured sweepingly out towards the lake, where sunshine glanced off the water, dappled this tree-girt clearing by the shore, indicating the absolute peace and quiet of the place.

She was still looking at him, but less uncertainly, as if his words were getting through to her. Then a frown creased her brow.

'But we've brought no provisions! And I've only got the clothes I'm standing up in!'

'Not exactly,' he said. 'Follow me.'

He headed back along the path to the SUV, pulling open the tailgate. As Lana caught up with him he heard her give what sounded like a choke.

'This should keep us going,' he said cheerfully, and lifted out a large cardboard carrier containing dry foods. It was stashed neatly next to a couple of cool boxes, a portable barbecue and several sacks of charcoal, and two small suitcases.

'One of the maids, Maria, packed some suitable gear for you while we were having dinner last night,' he informed Lana, 'and you can always borrow some of my stuff. I'll take this to the chalet—can you manage one of the cool boxes?'

He set off, relieved that she was not objecting. That, with this impulsive decision he'd made to get away from Rome, away from the *palazzo*, he might, finally, be getting it right with her. The way he wanted it to be.

Lana hefted up one of the cool boxes. Maybe Salvatore was right. Maybe it would be good not to have to put on any kind of front at all—not even to the *palazzo* staff. She'd felt awkward, having them treat her as the *signora*, even more than having his friends and acquaintances think she was. Now she could have a break from it.

Inside the chalet Salvatore was unpacking the groceries, stashing them away in the wooden cupboards above the sink. It made him look very domesticated. Not the powerful businessman or the lordly *signor* of a *palazzo*. It was, she found herself thinking, reassuring...

'Do I leave the cold stuff in the cool box?' Lana asked.

'No, there's a fridge—the chalet has solar-powered electricity and, you'll be pleased to know, running water, fed by a spring from further up the hill. The bathroom, such as it is, is just behind the kitchen.'

Lana peeked through a half-open door, seeing a very simple shower room with toilet facilities that she would be glad of.

'We've got cylinder gas to cook on, plus the barbecue, and oil lamps and candles to supplement the solar electric lights,' Salvatore was saying now. 'Okay, let's get the rest of the stuff from the car.'

It took a couple more trips to empty the boot, then they were done.

'Coffee?' asked Salvatore, lighting the gas hob as Lana climbed, somewhat gingerly, down the ladder from the mezzanine. There had just about been space up there to place her small suitcase on the wooden floor and check to see what Maria had packed for her. Shorts, cotton trousers, tee shirts, a jumper or two, another pair of canvas flat-soled shoes, some underwear, a swimsuit—that was about it.

No nightwear, she noted with sudden suspicion. And then realised that Maria had correctly assumed that her glamorous satin pyjamas were hardly suited to roughing it in a primitive lakeside chalet. Well, she would wear a tee shirt instead. And she would sleep, *quite* definitely, on her own, up there on the mezzanine. She could even pull up the ladder to repel boarders if need be—

But she was given no cause to do so. No such attempt was made. And when Lana finally climbed up the ladder, bidding goodnight to Salvatore, who was stretching himself out on the comfortable settee below, she knew she was glad he had brought her here.

Glad that here, away from absolutely everyone else, they could—just as he'd told her—be themselves.

Not a married couple in a totally unreal marriage made for completely non-romantic reasons that has had its end date written into a contract from the off. Not pretending to people that it's a real marriage, made for the reasons a marriage should be made.

While they were here they could put all that aside. 'Chillax' and be comfortable. Just as Salvatore was urging her to be.

Certainly the rest of the day had been relaxing. After they'd unpacked and had a cup of coffee out on the veranda they'd gone for an exploratory walk along the shore. The narrow path wound along the lake's edge, with more paths leading off it, up into the mixed deciduous and evergreen forest on the steep hillside. They'd returned as dusk gathered, and Salvatore had lit the log burner more for cosiness than warmth, before making dinner.

It had been a simple affair—pasta in a *ragu* out of a bottle, with parmesan grated by Salvatore—washed down by a robust red. Dessert had been a chocolate cake freshly baked at the *palazzo*, rich with icing. They'd eaten in front of the fire, then finished off the bottle of red wine playing board games they'd found in a cupboard, before going out to look at the lake in the starlight. A crescent moon had just been clearing the hills, thin in the heavens.

But Salvatore had made no attempt to take advantage of her. Scrupulously he had kept two metres from her as they'd paused to listen to the owls hooting in the distance, and they had not stayed out long. Back indoors, they'd time-sliced on the bathroom facilities, and Lana had just clambered up to the mezzanine to hurriedly tug on the longest tee shirt she could find by way of night attire, while Salvatore took his place in the bathroom.

She was asleep before he emerged.

She awoke to the aroma of coffee from the kitchenette below, and Salvatore bidding her to come down for breakfast. Pulling on shorts and a fresh tee, and a pair of canvas shoes, plaiting her hair into a long tail, she shinned down the ladder to see Salvatore, in a checked shirt, jeans and trainers, frying bacon and tomatoes, and toasting rolls out of a packet.

Again, just as he had the previous day, he struck her as being surprisingly domesticated. Reassuringly so.

He turned and smiled at her. 'Sleep well?' he asked.

'Like a log,' she answered. 'How about you?'

'Another log,' he assured her, then suggested she laid the outdoor table, bathed in warm sunshine already.

Ten minutes later they were seated, demolishing a hearty breakfast.

He was easy company, obviously relaxed and obviously cheerful, talking about what they might do on this their first day here. They decided on an easy hike up into the forest, in green and dappled shade, which they did, not talking much, for it would have spoilt the wooded quietness all around them.

They descended back to the cabin for a lunch of ham, salami and strong cheese, with tomatoes and peaches and thick-cut bread—eaten, like breakfast, outdoors—and Salvatore, Lana discovered, had plans for the afternoon.

'The chalet comes with a rowing boat,' he told her.

It was pulled up just beyond the solar panels, and also came with fishing tackle. Salvatore, it seemed, was an enthusiastic fisherman.

Lana made no objection to lolling back in the rowing boat when he shipped oars and dropped his line, waiting for a bite at the bait. She did object, however, to gutting the fish after he'd despatched them with a sharp but swift blow to the head against the gunwale.

Watching him deftly make them barbecue-ready with a couple of neat knife-thrusts, she found it hard to think of him as either a high-powered businessman or the elegant man-about-town of elite Roman society.

'So, where did you learn to gut fish, then?' she enquired lazily, glancing at him curiously.

'My father,' he replied.

For a moment she thought he was not going to say any more. Then he did. Looking out over the sunlit lake as he spoke.

'He took me fishing sometimes. At sea—off his motorboat. We'd drop anchor and spend the afternoon and evening out on the water. He didn't talk much, but I didn't mind. It was good just to be with him. It didn't happen very often. Nor did the fishing expeditions. He only took time off when his life got too complicated—even for him.'

Salvatore hadn't tensed, but there was an acerbic tinge to his voice now.

'Complicated?' Lana echoed.

It seemed strange to think of Salvatore as a young boy. A boy with, it seemed, complications in his family.

'My father,' he said, his tone still acerbic as he looked away over the lake, 'would sometimes set up a new mistress without informing the current incumbent—who would then kick off. So he would take off out to sea, where neither could get at him, while they fought it out between themselves.'

She was silent a moment, and so was he. Then... 'It must have been difficult for you,' she said quietly. For all their wealth, his had not been a happy family. It saddened her to think so, to think of him growing up in that way.

His head turned, dark eyes going to her. They were shadowed, and she knew instinctively that he was veiling what he was feeling. That was something she knew all about. She, too, had learnt to hide her tearing grief at her parents' dreadful death.

'Not nearly as difficult as it was for my mother,' he said.

With a sudden gesture, he flung the extracted innards of the fish he'd caught out into the lake water. Then, dropping the gutted fish into the plastic box he'd brought for the purpose and rinsing his hands, he looked at Lana.

'Theirs,' he told her, looking straight at her again, with a shadow deep in his dark eyes, his voice clipped, 'you will appreciate, was not a happy marriage.'

Her eyes filled with open sympathy. 'It can't have been.' She shook her head. 'It must have taken its toll on you, too.'

He gave a shrug. 'I survived.' He looked away again, back over the dark lake water with its hidden depths below the sunlight glancing off its surface, frowning perhaps against its brightness—or for another reason. 'Yet despite all the unhappiness my father caused my mother I still loved him.'

His words came from deep within. She knew it, understood it. Without realising it, she stretched her hand out, just touched his, as if to comfort him.

'It's natural to do so,' she said, her voice low. 'Children hate to take sides when there's dissent between parents.'

He looked back at her. 'Oh, I took sides, all right! My mother's—she was the injured party. But...' His expression changed. 'I also knew my father should never have married. Not just never have married my mother, but never married at all.' His voice hardened. 'He wasn't cut out for it.'

'Why did he?' Lana heard herself ask carefully.

It was strange to be hearing such intimate things about him—and yet out here, in the middle of the lake, just the two of them in the little rowing boat, so isolated from the rest of the world, maybe it was not so strange...

'He fell for my mother—big-time,' Salvatore answered her. 'The trouble was—' he gave a shake of his head '—what he really wanted was just an affair with her—nothing as permanent as marriage. But she came from a family where that sort of thing wasn't approved of, so they got married instead.'

Now there was a hollow in his voice that Lana could hear distinctly.

'She went on loving him all the time. Even when he'd got tired of her devotion.' He took a breath, and his gaze slipped out over the water. 'He was never actively hostile to her, simply chronically unfaithful. Indifferent to her. Never around much. He never wanted a divorce—it would have been difficult, anyway—and he stayed with her for my sake, too. He simply wanted to be able to…to play around the way he liked. Enjoyed. It was all he was capable of.'

Again, Lana was silent a moment. Then… 'My parents were very happy together,' she said. 'I took it for granted. But it's only when you realise that isn't always the case that you truly value it.'

He looked at her. 'They were lucky. So were you.'

She nodded. 'Yes—they were lucky in each other. Lucky in love. They chose wisely. I only wish that I had been as—'

She broke off. Salvatore looked at her questioningly. She made a painful face.

'I only wish I'd been as wise around Malcolm,' she said. 'But I know with hindsight that I just wanted someone in my life after my parents were killed—someone to make me feel less alone.' She took a breath. 'That makes me sound pathetic, I know.'

Salvatore's dark eyes rested on her. 'It makes you sound human,' he said. 'And he's out of your life now—and you're well rid of him!'

He reached for the shipped oars and dipped them into the lake water, starting to pull towards the shore, the muscles in his bare arms flexing as he pulled the boat through the water with apparently effortless strokes. Lana tried not to be conscious of his powerful physique, focussing instead on the approaching shoreline.

His words echoed in her head.

'He's out of your life...'

One day Salvatore would be out of her life too...

The thought seemed to pluck at her. The time would come when she was back in England, picking up her real life again. A thousand miles and more away from here.

A thousand miles and more away from Salvatore.

Her eyes went back to him and she wondered why the thought was unwelcome to her.

Wondered why she was thinking it at all.

'Time for a swim before our sundowner?' Salvatore enquired of Lana as she stepped out from the chalet, a bowl of freshly chopped salad in her hands.

They'd beached the rowing boat and he'd taken the fish indoors to the fridge, got the barbie going while Lana prepared the salad.

His answer was a shake of her head and a rueful laugh. 'No, thanks—I felt the water from the boat, and it's freezing!'

He gave a grin. 'All the more exhilarating!' he told her.

It did not change her mind, and with a laugh he

stripped off to his trunks and plunged into the lake. It was indeed very cold, but he struck out in a fast, powerful crawl, warming up as he did so. Reaching the middle of the lake, he duck-dived and headed back, emerging with his whole body glowing.

'Wild swimming!' he exclaimed. 'Nothing to beat it!'

He seized up his towel, patting himself dry. Aware that Lana's eyes were on him, though only sideways. Aware that he was glad they were. For all her strictures that night when he'd succumbed to kissing her under the stars, she could not shut down her natural response to him.

But it must be what she *wants—what* she *accepts. She has to accept that the reason for our marriage, the financial benefit it will bring her in the end, has no role to play in what is between us!*

To him it was very simple. Their marriage, although legal, was an irrelevance.

As marriage was to my father.

Affairs were all his father had ever wanted.

As do I.

His eyes shadowed.

I am my father's son.

He tossed the damp towel aside on to a chair, his mood darkening suddenly. Yes, he knew that! And he must remember it, too.

His eyes went to Lana. In shorts and tee shirt, her hair in a long plait, not a scrap of make-up, she looked every bit as radiantly beautiful as she did wearing a couture gown and diamonds.

Nothing can dim her beauty—lessen her allure. She is as desirable now as she was when I first saw her, wanting her from the first...

She had picked up the towel, was shaking it out and draping it neatly over the veranda balustrade so it would start to dry out. It was a simple, housewifely gesture, as if she had done it a hundred times for him. As if they were an established couple. It was a strange thought. At odds with what he'd just reminded himself of. The fact that transient affairs were all he wanted. That there was nothing else it was safe for him to want.

She was smiling reprovingly at him. 'It won't dry in a crumpled heap!' she reprimanded him with mock sternness.

'Mea culpa,' he acknowledged in a penitential tone, accepting her just criticism.

'Go and shower,' she told him. 'Then we can have our sundowners and you can get on with grilling that fish you caught! I'm starving! You must be too, after that freezing swim!'

He gave a laugh, agreeing with her, and headed off into the bathroom. Hunger growled in him. And not just for his supper.

For much, much more.

But exactly for what, he was no longer sure.

Their sundowners were nothing more sophisticated than a bottle of beer each, not even poured into glasses. From time to time Salvatore tested the barbecue, turning the potatoes to cook them evenly. Slices of red pepper stood ready, beside the waiting fish. The salad was dressed, and a packet of roasted nuts decanted into a plastic bowl, each of them having a packet of crisps to graze on as well.

Eventually Salvatore declared the moment right for grilling the peppers and fish, and proceeded to do so.

'For a man who enjoys the finest things in life,' Lana heard herself observe, humour in her voice, 'you're really very domesticated when you put your mind to it!'

He turned, giving a laugh. 'Do you think me one of those pampered playboys who fall apart if there's no one around to chef for them?' he riposted. 'I'm not quite so feeble, thank you!'

'No, but you're used to luxury,' she replied. 'Your world is so completely different from mine—'

He left the fish grilling, sitting down again and reaching for his beer, taking a mouthful.

'We're just people, Lana—you and I both. We're not so different.'

There was a smile in his voice, in his eyes—but there was more than just a smile in his eyes. Something that made her drop her own for a moment.

'We have a lot in common, really,' she heard him muse, and her gaze went back to him. He'd replaced his beer bottle on the table, was looking across the small wooden table at her. 'We have both had to survive tragedy, the untimely loss of our parents in traumatic circumstances. We've both agreed that marrying each other as we have, for very specific reasons, is not as insane as it might sound to others!'

There was a wry note in his voice at that, but then he went on, eyes holding hers.

'And we get on with each other well. We do, you know. It's easy for us to be in each other's company—I find it so, and I don't believe you don't. Look how we've got on when it comes to traipsing around the glories of Tuscany—and how well we're getting on here, now!'

He smiled again, warmth in his face, in his deep, dark eyes.

'Today has been good, hasn't it?' He gestured around him expansively. 'Basic this place might be, but what more do we need?' He lifted his beer bottle again, tilting it towards her. 'Let's drink to this place, shall we—because it's doing us both good?'

It was impossible to disagree with anything he'd said.

We do get on well—whether we're at the palazzo, or out sightseeing, or just chillaxing here in this uber-peaceful spot...

She wondered whether she should worry at it—but didn't. She just accepted it instead. It seemed the natural thing to do.

She made a wry face, tapping her beer bottle against his and taking a mouthful as he did, returning his *'Saluti!'* with a more British 'Cheers!'

Then the aroma from the barbecue distracted them, and Salvatore was standing up, removing the now nicely crisped fish and roasted peppers, plating them up. Then scooping up the soft-baked potatoes, putting one each on their plates.

Lana cut hers open, dropping a generous helping of butter into the steaming centre. Appetite speared within her. They settled down to eat companionably, both heartily tucking in to the simple but highly tasty supper.

We do get on well...he's right. And for people with such different backgrounds, we have more in common than one might suppose.

Her eyes rested on him as he reached for another beer, flicking open the top with practised ease, before taking a swallow straight from the bottle. In the dusk, and in the soft light from the storm lantern hanging from the balustrade over the veranda, the planes of his face were accentuated by the shadows cast on it. Enhancing—if enhancement were possible at all, she thought, giving an unconscious inner sigh—the sculpted perfection that was his.

He lowered his bottle, catching her gaze on him, slanting a smile at her. Something flickered in his eyes—something that seemed to quicken her pulse— but then his long lashes swept down, veiling it from her. But she had seen enough. He might be sticking to what he'd promised her that night after Florence, but she could not deny—however much she might wish to do so—the other searing and undeniable truth about what they shared in common...

The fact that, for all the complications between them, all the impossibility of what he wanted, their desire was as undeniable as it was unsuppressed.

She gave another sigh, inwardly this time. Knowing, as she dropped her gaze, that it was tinged with regret...

Regret for what surely was too impossible, too complicated to yield to...

* * *

'Ever rowed a boat before?' Salvatore was asking. 'No? Okay, so I'll teach you.'

He got her seated on the bench, an oar in either hand, and pushed the little craft out into deeper water before vaulting lightly in himself. Then he focussed on getting Lana to angle the oars correctly, before attempting to head off.

'Not bad,' he said approvingly as she did as he bade her. 'Shall we see if we can make it to the far side of the lake? See what's over there?'

They did, and beached beside a rocky promontory which afforded them a perch on which to eat the picnic lunch they'd made after breakfast. Then they strolled off along another lakeside footpath, meandering along its gentle contours.

The day was passing easily, companionably. Salvatore was glad of it. Glad of a great deal.

Glad of that covert look she threw me last night, brief though it was.

But he would not—could not—rush her. Or pressurise her. It must come from her, the decision that he so wanted her to make. It must be right for her—completely right.

So that she can accept what is between us.

His eyes went to her as they settled themselves back in the rowing boat, with Salvatore doing the rowing this time. She sat back, hands resting widely on the gunwale on either side of her, lifting her beautiful face to the sunshine streaming down out of a cloudless sky, warm after the cool of the forest.

He felt something move within him, something he did not recognise.

How beautiful she is! How perfect—

Dimly, he knew that surely his desire for her would eventually pall, as all his affairs palled.

Just as my father's did.

No, he would not think about his father—about the serial womanising he'd spent his life pursuing. Never wanting to fall in love with anyone. *While the one woman who'd loved him he ignored. Left to pine, hopelessly, for him. A man who never loved her.*

He pulled his thoughts away from that, too. It was too painful. He'd witnessed his mother's pain at her husband's rejection of her, his indifference to her.

His gaze refocussed on Lana, drinking in her loveliness as he rowed her back to the simple chalet he'd brought her to. Would its peaceful remoteness, these peaceful days he was spending with her, far away from the world that had pressed upon them, bring him what he longed for?

He did not know. He could only hope.

And hope, for now, would have to do.

CHAPTER NINE

LANA FORKED THE last of the melt-in-the-mouth barbecued lamb fillet—richly marinaded since that morning
with garlic, lemon and rosemary—and gave a sigh of
repletion as she cleared her plate. It had been another
good day of taking their ease in this beautiful remote
spot. And another mouth-watering barbecue this evening, shared with Salvatore as she had shared the day
with him.

'I hope you've left room for the roasted bananas.' He
smiled at her, his own plate already empty. 'A shame
we have no *gelato* to go with them, but the chalet
doesn't run to a freezer. We'll make do with cream
from the fridge instead. And douse them in amaretto
for sweetness.'

They did, too, and as ever Lana lingered over the
sheer luxury of eating guilt-free desserts. Around them
night thickened, and the sound of owls haunted the forest around them. They were cocooned in the light from
the oil lamp, which was throwing Salvatore's striking
features into yet more striking *chiaroscuro*.

Lana was all too aware that she should suppress the

thought, but it seemed too much effort. Her arms, her pecs and quads were tired from the unaccustomed exertion of rowing across the lake, and all she wanted to do was rest and relax. Not to make any effort. It would be an effort not to let herself do what she always seemed to want to do—let her eyes go to the man opposite her. The way they had right from the first...

Lingering over the glass of amaretto Salvatore had poured for her, in addition to dousing the barbecued bananas in it, feeling the rich liqueur's sweetness in her veins, she gave herself up to the indulgence of letting her gaze go where it wanted. It seemed easier, less effort, to do so.

They were no longer on the wooden chairs at the table below the veranda, next to the barbecue, but had repaired with their liqueurs to the bench on the veranda itself, padded with cushions filched from the settee. They sat there, not touching, keeping a space between them. The lightest of night breezes winnowed across the lake, refracting the starlight. The moon was riding high, silvering the dark waters of the lake. It was peaceful—balmy, even—and, replete and content, she went on gazing placidly out over the unchanging scene, catching the scent of the pine trees, the deep, earthy green smell of the forest all around, savouring the sweet, strong, almond liqueur warming her throat as it slid down in tiny sips.

Salvatore's long legs were stretched out in front of him and his head was turned towards her. He'd finished his amaretto, set the glass down on the veranda floor, under the bench. He was looking across at her.

'Another good day?' he asked.

She could hear the smile in his voice.

'Another good day,' she agreed.

She took another sip of her liqueur. It was sweet and warm in her veins. She let her gaze play on his face, knowing she wanted to, knowing she should not, half veiling her eyes and knowing she should make some remark about being tired after a good but long day, go inside, climb the ladder to her private bed.

Knowing that she should not go on sitting there, a mere cushion's space between them, while the wind blew across the dark lake and the moon dipped down towards the canopy of the trees on the far shore, painting the world with silver.

Knowing the veiling of her eyes did not disguise the fact that she was gazing at him, drinking him in as he sat there, his cuffs turned back, the vee of his throat exposed to the night air, the planes of his face perfected by the low light that touched the sable of his hair with gold.

Knowing he knew that she was gazing at him… That she could not help but do so.

For how could she help it? The question shaped in her head hopelessly, helplessly. She had always wanted to gaze at him. From the very first.

But I fought it—I fought it because…because…

Why had she fought it? There were reasons, she knew. Reasons she had run from him that night after Florence. Reasons she had told herself that his kiss at the Duchessa's had been for show only. Reasons she had insisted their strange marriage be entirely celibate.

Reasons. Complications…

I married for money—so I can't confuse why I married with all that I feel and want and yearn for…

Could she?

Here, away from the watching world, it was just him and her. Here, they were not some fictitious man and wife. Here, they were only man and woman. And very, very real…

Thoughts, feelings, longings rippled within her like currents of water…flowing in complicated eddies… finding no outlet. Another owl hooted, a breath of moving air rippled the lake water, a fish splashed far out in the centre of the lake then was gone.

'So, what are we to do, hmm?'

Salvatore's low voice broke the silence lapping all around them. His eyes were meeting hers, holding hers. She felt the breath still in her throat, her eyes searching his as if looking for the meaning in the words he'd just spoken. Words that echoed the confusion in her own mind.

But she knew their meaning. Knew it even before he reached his hand towards her in the shadowed light, meshing their fingers. She felt the strength of his, their warmth twining with hers. His eyes were still holding hers.

'Can you truly not see how very simple this is?' he asked her.

His voice was husky and it did things to her…things that echoed the sweet warmth of the almond liqueur, the warm pulse of her blood. Her gaze searched his almost pleadingly. The pulse of her blood grew stronger, her breath shallower. His strong fingers meshed so easily with hers…

'But it isn't,' she answered him, her voice low. Pained. 'It isn't simple at all!'

He shook his head. 'It is,' he contradicted her. 'So very simple.'

He drew a breath, inhaling slowly, never letting go of her eyes, his fingers tightening on hers, the thumb lying across her palm moving slightly, so very slightly, across its surface. His voice, when he spoke, was lower than hers, and still more husky. His gaze was intense, holding hers.

'Here…now…our marriage is very far away. And why we married—the reasons for it, so particular only to ourselves—are very far away too. Do not think about them—they have no place here. No relevance. They have nothing at all to do with what is happening between us! What has been there from the start. You have always known it—you know it now. What is here now has always been here. It is between *us*, you and me, the attraction we have felt for each other every day!'

A smile, half-rueful, half-sensuous, played about his mouth.

'Had we never married we would still be here, in Italy, under the stars,' he said. 'I would have come back for you even if I hadn't needed to do anything about Giavanna and her father! I would have come back, Lana.'

She felt him lift her hand…lift it and graze it softly, sensuously, with his mouth. It was like the touch of silk velvet.

'For you.'

His eyes were pouring into hers like wine she could not resist, and nor did she wish to. She could feel her blood singing in her veins, the breath catching in her throat.

'I would have come back, my most *bellissima* Lana, to make you mine. As I do now.' His eyes were holding hers…a silken noose. 'If you will have me,' he said.

He leant towards her and she caught the scent of his masculinity, potent and seductive…oh, so seductive… as his mouth found hers. Her eyelids fluttered shut. She gave herself up to the sensation. Could not help but give herself to it, so gentle, so arousing. It melted something within her. Something that had been knotted tightly… that confusing, complicated mesh that had bound her, trapped her, since the moment she had agreed to undertake their strange marriage.

Was she confusing money with desire?

But the money goes with the marriage. The desire is only within ourselves—

She heard his words in her head again—saying that even had he not needed to make their strange marriage he still would have come back to her. To make her his.

And I would have gone to him—I know that. I would have lain down my burden of endless work to try and pay my mortgage—would have thrown in the towel, accepted the loss Malcolm has imposed on me. Accepted, too, what flared between me and Salvatore from the very first time I set eyes on him.

She felt her mind move, her thoughts taking her to the place she knew she was meant to be.

I accept it now.

He drew away from her, but only a fraction, his eyes in the dim light warm and intimate.

'So will you?' His low voice was a question. 'Will you have me? Just as I am—just as you are? Here, now, under the stars? In this quiet and private place?'

He smiled, warm and intimate, like his eyes still holding hers, searching hers.

'It is so very, very simple. That we desire each other—'

His mouth found hers again, as softly sensual as before, tasting her lips for longer this time, not releasing her. And she did not want him to. Did not want to do anything but give herself to the moment, to the sensuous arousal he was inciting in her. She tried to think why it was that she should not be kissing him, but it was impossible. Impossible to do anything but yield to him, to let him part her lips, deepen his kiss, tighten his clasp on her hand pressed between them.

A million nerve-endings were firing in her, and the sweetness of his touch was melting her again. And then he was lifting his mouth away, gazing down at her with a rueful half smile playing on his lips.

'So what are we going to do, Lana? We're here, in this beautiful space, alone together, under the night. We desire each other. It is truly as simple as that.'

He held on to her hand, their fingers still meshed, as he drew back from her.

'This is a simple place, Lana, for simple truths.' He gestured all around him. 'It's why I brought you here. Away from anything that's complicated. That you think is complicated.'

He smiled an inviting smile, meeting her eyes, now lifted helplessly to his.

'This has been waiting to happen right from the first. We have both known it. And now…here…is the time.'

He brushed her lips with his again, lightly, softly, then drew back, taking her empty glass from her nerveless fingers to place it beside his own. Then he drew her to her feet.

As his eyes held hers, never letting them go, she felt the pulse at her throat thudding, the haze in her mind filling it. Beyond him, the dark waters of the lake stretched to the unseen forest beyond. It was so quiet, so far away from everything.

Just us—just here. Together.

And suddenly out of nowhere, rippling through her like the night breeze in the conifers all around, she knew that that was what she wanted. She heard his words again—*'So simple…so very simple…'*

And that was what it was. As simple as the moonlight silvering the lake, the sweet night air, the call of owls in the forest, the quietness all around them.

So very simple.

He said nothing, and nor did she. There was no need to. And that, too, was very simple.

As simple as going indoors.

His hand still holding hers.

The mezzanine bed took them into its close confines and they took each other into an embrace. He laid her down upon it, and she was pliant in the soft lowering of her willing body. The light was very dim up here, but she did not need light to know him—to find him with her hands lifted to his chest, pressed against its muscled wall as he leaned over her. His body was warm and firm, and she could feel the contours of his ribs through the material of his shirt.

Her fingers found the buttons, slipped them one by one. He let her do it, smiling down at her, his hands planted either side of her head as, little by little, she revealed his body to her, slowly, carefully, sliding the shirt from his shoulders.

He shrugged it off, discarding it. 'Now my turn,' he said. He was smiling, his eyes holding hers, his gaze intimate and warm.

He eased her tee shirt from her, lifting it at her waist to slide it upward. She wore no bra—not here in the forest—and as the high, small mounds of her breasts were exposed she heard him catch his breath.

'*Por Dio,* but you are so beautiful!' It was a sigh. An exhalation. A homage.

She felt his head lower—felt, with a rush of sweet pleasure, his mouth close over one breast. Felt it flower beneath his ministrations, its sensitivity increased a hundredfold, a thousandfold. She arched her neck in pleasure, offering herself to him, first one breast and then the other.

Then he was pulling away from her. She gave a cry of protest, but all he was doing was rapidly and purposefully shedding the rest of his clothes.

And hers.

And then he was coming down over her, and the weight of his body was on hers, his mouth seeking hers, finding it as her mouth opened to his, velvet upon velvet.

Her hands reached around the strong column of his back, glorying in its sculpted contours as his kiss deepened. She gave a sudden gasp of realisation. And glorying in the strength of his arousal, pressing against her.

Excitement quickened within her, an answering arousal, and heat beating up from the core of her body, flushing through her. She gave a low moan and then his mouth was leaving hers, sliding down the shallow valley between her ripened breasts, down over the sleek smoothness below…and further yet.

She gave a soft cry, eyes widening, as his hands lowered to her waist. His own body was arching now, to give him access to what he wanted…

Her thighs slackened. It was impossible to resist, because resisting—oh, dear God—was the very last thing she wanted to do. It was impossible not to want what he was doing now…not to want the incredible, delicate, tantalising, exquisitely arousing sensations he was drawing from her. They mounted and mounted and mounted. She felt the heat within her rise. The pleasure he was giving her was so intense, so incredible, that surely it was impossible that it should exist at all.

She felt her body melt, her head roll back, low moans breaking from her throat. She said his name,—an invocation…a plea. And at his name he lifted away, his hands sliding around her hips, tilting them upwards, opening her to him…

To his possession.

His complete possession.

She gave a gasp, a cry, her hands folding over his shoulders as his mouth found hers again, tasting and melding and fusing…even as his body melded and fused with hers.

He moved within her and she was folding around him, possessing him even as he was possessing her, and her body was melting…melting…

And then—as his slow, expert, ever-deepening thrusts within her aroused silken tissues brought her closer and closer still to what she ached for, to what she craved, what she sought with all her throbbing being—like molten metal her body became one single, all-consuming white-hot fusion with his.

She was drawing him deeper, closer, feeling her throbbing tissues convulse around him as wave after wave of a pleasure she had never known existed, never known *could* exist overwhelmed her. And she was crying out, her fingers clutching at him, clinging to him, clinging to his body now surging within her. And now it was him crying out, head bowed, low and urgent and guttural, as his moment came, matching hers as they were both fused in absolute union.

Her sated body gave one last long convulsion around him and then she was drawing his body down to hers, cradling it in her embracing arms, holding him within her, her heart hammering against his. Exhaustion swept over her, but her body was glowing in the flame, heat still in her tissues, ripples of pleasure still going through her. She did not want to let him go…did not want to lose him…could not bear to do so.

She wrapped her arms more tightly around him and he held her close against him, limbs meshed, their heartbeats gradually slowing. He was murmuring to her...soft words, sweet words...in his native language, his mouth gently kissing the column of her throat, holding her close in his arms. So very close.

It was the only place in all the world she wanted to be.

It was, she knew with absolute certainty as they held each other, as simple as that.

Salvatore turned to smile at Lana, his fishing line now cast, as the little boat bobbed gently on the lake water. She was lolling back, legs outstretched, one bare foot resting on his thigh with intimate, easy relaxation. She smiled when he smiled at her. An intimate, easy smile.

Idly, he wondered whether it might be possible to make love to her in the boat while waiting for the fish to bite.

As though reading his mind, Lana turned her smile to a laugh.

'No—don't even think of it!' she warned. 'I do *not* want to end up in that freezing cold water because we've rocked the boat too much! Wait till we get back to shore!'

'How do you know what I was thinking?' he asked with an answering laugh.

Her eyes glinted. 'Female intuition,' she said.

He slid his hand around her bare foot, lifting it to drop a light kiss on the slender arch. Even her feet were the most beautiful he'd ever seen.

Everything about her is the most beautiful! Everything...

Including, most of all, the way she had given herself to him. Given in to what had been between them from the first. To what was now flourishing like a glorious flower opening to the warmth of the sun...

He let his lashes dip down over his eyes as he released her foot, which once again rested on his thigh. It was a dangerous place for it to rest, and he told her so.

'You might find I suddenly lose interest in fishing,' he warned her.

'I'll take that as a compliment,' she teased. 'Me versus fishing...hmm, tough call...'

'No competition,' he informed her. 'It's fishing every time.'

It was a lie. A blatant lie. And she knew it. It would have been impossible for her not to. In the remoteness of the log cabin they could do as they pleased, when they pleased—and it pleased him very much to demonstrate, comprehensively, just how much he desired her.

She was all that he had thought she would be, had known she would be. And more.

Much more.

Had he ever known a woman like her? It was a stupid question—one that had only one answer. An answer he did not need to give even to himself.

All he had to give himself was what there was between them. Now, here in this lakeside idyll, and way beyond. At the *palazzo*, in Rome, on business trips—it didn't matter. Lana would be with him by day and, of absolute certainty, by night. In his arms. His bed.

Just as he had wanted from the first. Married or not married—nothing would change that.

Lana glanced around her bedroom. It seemed strange to come back to the *palazzo* after their lakeside idyll. More complicated. Outwardly, nothing had changed, and yet everything had changed. Self-consciousness burned in her, as though all the household staff could see how very different things were now between her and Salvatore. But the only real change was that the communicating door between her bedroom and Salvatore's was now unlocked.

Yet for all that had changed between them since their stay at the lakeside chalet, one thing had not. Whenever a member of staff addressed her as *signora*, treating her as though she were mistress here, she still felt a fake. A fraud. Here under false pretences.

Her expression flickered as she stood looking out over the wide, beautiful gardens. Salvatore had said it was simple, their desire for each other—a desire they consummated night after night. But how could it be simple when the world thought their marriage real? When they themselves knew the truth? Knew that it was not designed to mean what marriage *should* mean—that it was not to last...was to end, before next spring turned to summer, in a divorce planned from the very outset.

She turned away from the window, her thoughts still troubled. And they would be more troubled yet, she knew. Today they were driving back to Rome. There were social engagements to attend, work meetings for Salvatore. Their honeymoon was over.

Except that it was never a honeymoon at all—because I am not a real wife to Salvatore. We are having an affair, that is all—whatever the world thinks, whatever his household here thinks, whatever his friends in Rome think.

She picked up her handbag, went downstairs. Salvatore was already in the car, waiting for her. She got in and he kissed her softly, eyes smiling.

'Looking forward to Rome?' he asked.

She bit her lip, unwilling to answer.

He started the engine and the car crunched slowly over the gravel towards the gilded gates beyond, now opening to let him pass.

'It will be easier for you this time,' he told her.

The expression in his eyes told her why he thought so. She wished she could agree with him. But it was impossible to do so.

So she said nothing. It seemed the easiest thing to do.

CHAPTER TEN

SALVATORE'S MOOD WAS good. It had never been better. It was impossible it should be otherwise. He had everything in the world he wanted. He had stopped Giavanna and Roberto in their ambitious tracks, his life was going just where he wanted, and right now that meant one thing only.

Lana...

Her name purred in his head. Her image was always there.

Beautiful, breathtaking—and *his*! Just as he had known she would be. Because how could it ever have been otherwise After desiring her so much?

It was impossible that such desire should have been denied any longer, for reasons that were as irrelevant as they were pointless. And hers was as strong as his—did he not know that now, with night after burning night in each other's arms?

The week they'd spent at the chalet by the lake had proved that completely. *He'd* proved it. And he would go on doing so now they were here in Rome as well. He was eager to show her off—not, this time, simply because she was a blocking move, to counter Giavanna and Roberto, but because he just wanted everyone to see him with her.

Why? Why do you want everyone to see you with her?

The question flickered in his head now, as he got out of the car, which then drove off into the busy Rome traffic, leaving Salvatore to stride the few paces to the fashionable bar where he was meeting Luc Dinardi.

Why? He answered his own question dismissively. Because he wanted to—that was all. He didn't have to justify it. Or explain it. Or even think about it. Let alone give any consideration to the fact that he'd never felt any need to show off the previous women in his life.

Well, he hadn't had to, had he? he thought impatiently. The women he'd had affairs with had come from the same social circles as himself—and in Rome everyone knew each other, and who was with who, or not. Whereas Lana was new to them.

But she's fitting in perfectly.

He'd already paid tribute to her in that first week of their marriage, telling her that she was playing Signora Luchesi flawlessly. And she still was. At all the glittering social events he had taken her to—showing her off—she'd been superb. She seemed to have made a hit with everyone—from his personal friends to old-school social arbiters such as the Duchessa, who had—as she had said she would that evening when Giavanna had shown off her spoilt brat credentials to perfection in chucking champagne over Lana—invited Lana to lunch. She was with the Duchess now, which was why he himself had agreed to meet up with Luc today.

He strode into the crowded bar, spotting Luc and heading towards him.

'Salva—*ciao*! It's good to see you again!' Luc greeted him warmly, with a cheerful slap on his shoulder. 'Let me look at you.' Eyes with a familiar worldly expression flicked over Salvatore. Then...

'Yes, marriage is definitely suiting you!' Luc said with an approving air, amusement in his voice. 'Who'd have thought?' he murmured, the amusement now more pronounced. 'Salvatore Luchesi—renowned bachelor of Rome, always playing the field—now a good and faithful husband!'

Salvatore tensed. 'Good and faithful' husbands did not run in the Luchesi family.

For a moment he felt an impulse to tell Luc the truth about Lana and himself—about the reason he'd married her. To disclaim any assumption that she was a permanent fixture in his life. But he bit his tongue. If he gave Luc any hint of the real reason for his marriage it would be all over Rome, courtesy of that one-woman gossip mill Stephanie, to whom Luc would be unable to resist passing on such a juicy morsel. And then it would reach Roberto and Giavanna, undoing all his efforts to get them off his case.

No, he had to keep up the fiction that Lana was going to stick around as his wife long-term.

Ruthlessly, he turned the tables on his friend, to avoid any further discussion of his own marriage, let alone the reason for it.

'And what about you, Luc? Are you ever going to make an honest woman of Stephanie?'

Luc gave a shrug. 'Oh, you know the score, Salva. She and I run around together when there's no one else for either of us. But it's out of habit as much as anything. I don't think anything will change. Well...' he made a face '...unless during one of our together periods she tells me she's pregnant, I guess!'

Salvatore looked at him. 'Would you know it was yours, though? Given your mutual lack of commitment to each other?'

Luc looked away for a moment, a strange expression on his face. 'That might not matter so much,' he said slowly.

Salvatore frowned. 'You'd raise another man's child?' His voice sharpened unconsciously.

'If the other man didn't want to be a father...then, yes, I possibly would. Unless, of course, Steph didn't want me any longer, only the other man.'

Salvatore took another mouthful of his martini. It tasted suddenly more sour than astringent. He put the glass back on the bar.

You're not wanted any longer...

The words echoed in his head. He knew the pain that could be inflicted when someone was told that.

'My darling boy, I have to accept—I have no choice but to accept—that your father simply does not want me any longer. Not in that way. As the mother to his son—yes, of course, and that will never change. But for himself? Ah, no, that has long gone.'

His father's rejection of his mother had hurt her so

deeply. He had seen it, witnessed it as a young teenager when he'd started to understand just how unhappy his mother had been made by his father's constant infidelities. Yet she had not wanted to end the marriage either. Not just because she would not break up the family, but because, he had come to realise, his mother had constantly hoped that one day his father would turn away from all his other women and come back to the woman who'd loved him through thick and thin.

Instead, what had awaited his parents had not been some fairy-tale joyous reconciliation but a devastating plane crash, cutting short their lives.

He pulled his mind away from such painful memories, realising that Luc was speaking to him.

'Talking of pregnancy, my old friend,' he was saying, looking straight at Salvatore, his voice half-humorous, half-cautious, 'you do realise that that was the suspicion Steph had about why you married so unexpectedly?'

'Absolutely not!' Salvatore refuted, tensing unconsciously.

He changed the subject decisively, to that of a recent football match, and Luc picked up the challenge for they supported opposing teams. With other sporting topics it served to take them through a long and convivial lunch.

Lana took a careful mouthful of her wine, conscious that she needed to be on her very best behaviour. She was lunching with the Duchessa in her private family apartments above the grandly magnificent *piano nobile*, where the charity fundraiser had been held.

The Duchessa was being very warm, very gracious, but she was also, Lana was aware, drawing her out. Thankfully, she seemed to accept at face level the fact that she and Salvatore had had a whirlwind romance and had acted on impulse, and there were no regrets.

'I am glad to hear it.' The Duchessa smiled. She looked directly at Lana. 'You are aware that Salvatore's parents were killed very tragically in a plane crash?'

Lana nodded. 'Yes, he has told me,' she said quietly. She took a low breath. 'Mine, too, were killed. In a car crash—'

'Ah,' said the Duchessa, and her eyes rested on Lana—she could almost feel it. A beringed hand was pressed lightly on hers in a sympathetic gesture. 'That is a bond between you indeed.'

Was it? Lana wondered. Her loss had driven her into the arms of Malcolm—an unwise reaction to the emptiness of her life. But her life was not empty any more. She had Salvatore—

She swallowed, her throat tight suddenly.

I've got him for a year, that's all. No more than that.

The Duchessa's hand was lifting from hers, and she was speaking again.

'Salvatore's mother was my goddaughter,' she was saying. 'She was very unhappy in her marriage.'

'He…he told me as much,' Lana replied.

'Yes. I've often thought that it was his father's philandering that made Salvatore avoid marriage,' the Duchessa mused. 'Because he did not want to risk discovering he was no better than his father.' Her voice changed. 'Which is why I am so glad that he has overcome that reluctance—thanks to you.'

Lana stayed silent. What could she say? She wished the Duchessa would stop talking about such things. They were really nothing to do with her. Discomfort filled her—both at the fact that she was being treated as though she were Salvatore's wife for real, and because it only emphasised to her that she was not.

I'm just his lover—his current lover.

Emotion twisted inside her. Though it should not.

I've known from the start how temporary our time is together.

He had been straight with her right from the off. Straight about the reasons he wanted them to marry and about when their marriage would end. Straight, too, about his desire for her. He had not deceived her in anything.

Malcolm had deceived her from the start—had had a malevolent hidden agenda up his thieving sleeve.

Salvatore's honesty set him totally apart from Malcolm. He was a far more worthwhile human being. One it would be very easy to come to feel more for than what held them to each other now merited...

She shied away from the thought—it was not a safe place for her mind to go.

What she had with Salvatore now was all she would ever have. She knew that—accepted it.

Because I must. Because his honesty from the start has spelled out all that we can ever be to each other. He's never pretended otherwise. I must be glad of that.

And yet gladness, suddenly, was not what she felt at all…

'You look troubled, my dear…'

The voice of the Duchessa pierced her thoughts—thoughts she did not want to have.

'But I am sure there is no need. Salvatore has eyes only for you!'

Lana's eyes veiled.

For now, yes.

For now, Salvatore was ardent in his attentions, his desires. But they had a shelf life—a time limit.

This time next year it will all be over. I shall be back in England, processing our divorce. Our pre-planned divorce.

How would that go down with his friends? His circle here in Rome? She didn't know. It was not her concern. Her only concern would be what she made of her life after Salvatore Luchesi had left it.

A sense of sudden bleakness filled her.

The Duchessa was changing the subject, saying something about an opera gala that was in the offing, and Lana was grateful. She could not take any more close examination of her marriage, her relationship with Salvatore, nor of her reactions to such examination.

Least of all any examination of those reactions…

'Have you been to New York often?' Salvatore asked, turning to Lana, sitting beside him in First Class, with an enquiring smile.

'Fashion Week—twice a year. So more often than I can count!' she answered.

She was glad to be accompanying Salvatore on a business trip. Glad to be out of Rome, where she was under constant surveillance, or so she uncomfortably felt, with everyone treating her as if she truly were the woman Salvatore Luchesi had chosen to be his wife—to make his life with— when she was no such thing at all.

It would be much easier being on her own with him, as they had been at the lakeside chalet. Far more honest. And after New York they would be flying down to the Bahamas.

'I want you all to myself again,' Salvatore had told her, his gaze warm and possessive.

'Me too,' she'd said, and smiled.

They got exactly that.

Their cabana at the exclusive resort opened onto a tiny secluded cove, private and for their own use, sheltered from the world by the palm trees waving in the cooling breeze. Their days were lazy, with their butler arriving on call with drinks, with gourmet meals, with anything they wanted.

But their wants were simple.

Each other.

Making love under the palm-thatched roof of their cabana. Making love in the plunge pool. Making love on the silver sand at midnight. Making love whenever desire swept over them and brought them into each other's arms, leaving them sated and fulfilled, still in each other's arms…

For Lana it was an ecstasy she had never thought possible. Had never thought existed. Malcolm, she now realised, had been incredibly selfish, pleasing only himself. Whereas Salvatore—

Sweet memory and eager anticipation mingled inside her like honey and cream…

In Salvatore's arms it was as if only they existed— nothing and no one else. Only the desire he aroused in her with the soft caresses of his hands, the skilled exploration of his fingertips, the velvet of his mouth, the lean strength of his body moving over hers…

Their limbs would mingle, her hands clutching his shoulders, her thighs winding around his, her spine arching. And then would come the low, pleading moans in her throat as he brought her ever nearer to that incredible, unbelievable moment when her blood would rush in her veins, her heart pounding as her body convulsed around his, and a tide of pleasure so exquisite she cried out would lift her to a heaven that she had never known existed—that could only exist in Salvatore's arms, in his strong embrace, in the passion of his desire for her. Of hers for him….

When she was lying in his arms, time stopped. All time. The sun rose and set and the days passed, slipping one by one into a past that existed as little as did the future.

She would not let there be a future. Not yet. Not when she wanted to embrace only the simplicity of what she had with Salvatore now, to embrace the bliss that came in his arms, the sense of ease and companionship that came just by being with him. The happiness…

They stood with their arms wound about each other on the silvered sand, still warm from the day's heat, watching the sun slip into the shallow turquoise sea, content to do nothing more than watch it set on another day of happiness.

And on their return to the *palazzo* they watched it set from the little stone gazebo at the far side of the garden, where once Lana had sat with her paperback, Salvatore still a stranger to her. He was a stranger no longer.

And they watched it set from halfway up a Swiss alp, when Salvatore took her with him on a business trip to Zurich. And then again from the penthouse suite of a high-rise hotel in Frankfurt… They watched as it bathed the Île de la Cité in Paris in golden light…watched it shine on the canals of Amsterdam and the lake of Geneva—wherever his business affairs took him.

There was only one business destination to which she declined to accompany him—London.

She would be there again soon enough…

When their sunsets had slipped from present into past.

She did not think about it. Would not. There was no point. She was with him now, sharing his life, his bed. When he no longer needed her to be his wife she would not be.

It was, after all, very simple.

Best to keep it that way.

The way Salvatore had told her it was.

* * *

Salvatore swung into the Viscari Roma, glad of the air-conditioning within. Rome in late summer was hot, and it felt even hotter after the rain London had been experiencing. He wished Lana had come with him, but she never came on his London trips.

'You only come abroad with me for the sightseeing!' he'd accused her with a laugh.

'I was never keen on London even when I had to live there,' she'd answered. 'I'll be selling up and moving out once I'm back in the UK permanently.'

He'd found himself frowning slightly at what she'd said. Then put it down to his disappointment that she didn't want to come with him. He didn't want to be away from her even for a handful of days.

And now he was back in Rome. He had flown in that very evening, in time to join Lana in celebrating Luc's birthday with a convivial dinner. It was to be here at the Viscari again, in the same private salon where he'd first introduced Lana to his friends in the spring.

He frowned again. Had so much time really passed since then? Had Lana really been part of his life that long already? It seemed to have flashed by.

Maybe, he thought, it was because disentangling his affairs from Roberto was proving easier than he'd been prepared for. And the main reason for that was that, far from obstructing him, Roberto was co-operating in the process.

For that, Salvatore thought cynically, he had Giavanna to thank. Thwarted in her ambitions for himself, she had set her sights on another prey. This time, much to her doting father's approval, the heir to a viscountcy. Salvatore wished them well of each other.

Now, making his way to the bar, where they were gathering before dinner, he let his eyes go straight to Lana, decorously sipping a cocktail, one fabulously long leg crossed elegantly over the other, looking, as ever, a complete knock-out in an iridescent mid-blue sheath that moulded her beautiful body. A stab of pride and proprietorship went through Salvatore, his eyes only for her.

And she had eyes only for him.

As she saw him her face lit, and she said his name in happy greeting. He kissed her cheeks, then greeted the others. Laura's pregnancy was advanced, and he could see Vito was being very protective of her.

Luc arrived shortly after, Stephanie with him, as exuberant as ever. She and Luc had had one of their periodic splits, each amusing themselves with a different partner, but were now back with each other again. It was a strange relationship, and one Salvatore could not fathom. The words Luc had said to him a while back came back into his head—that he would be prepared to stand by Stephanie if she ever got pregnant by a man who didn't want her. What would persuade a man to do that?

He gave a mental shrug, setting aside such a personally irrelevant question, settling down to an enjoyable evening.

A decisive glint formed in his eyes as he ran them

over Lana. She was more beautiful than ever. Her figure, now that her model's ultra-low-calorie diet was long gone, was more rounded now, deliciously curvaceous in all the right places. He could not wait to celebrate his return to Italy that night with her...

Lana stepped out of the ferociously expensive famous-name boutique in the Via dei Condotti, and stopped short.

'Lana, *ciao*! Been spending more of Salvatore's money? What gorgeous gowns have you bought this time?'

The voice greeting her was friendly, the question humorously expressed, but Lana could hear the barb in it. And she wasn't surprised. The person hailing her on the pavement was Giavanna Fabrizzi.

Lana schooled her expression into one of politeness. 'Hello, Giavanna,' she said in a friendly enough tone.

'You can wish me happy,' Giavanna announced, holding up her hand with an air of triumph to show off an engagement ring. 'It's been in Ernesto's family for centuries,' Giavanna confided with an air of smugness 'Every *viscontessa* has worn it—I shall be the next.'

Lana's smile was genuine. 'I'm really glad you've found your happy ending,' she said.

Giavanna smiled at her. Did the smile reach her eyes? Lana wasn't sure. She remained wary of the girl, for all her apparent friendliness now.

'Just like you did,' said Giavanna. 'And,' she added, 'that ex of yours.'

Lana tensed. Giavanna was lifting her phone out of her handbag, bringing up a photo.

'He certainly got lucky!' Giavanna was saying, holding up her phone for Lana to see.

Her eyes went to the photo, clearly from some celebrity's website. It was of one of Hollywood's top female movie stars, and at her side was Malcolm. Looking more handsome than ever. Bleached blond, and with a blinding smile of newly capped and whitened teeth. Looking incredibly pleased with himself.

The text below leapt out at her. The dominating phrase was: *Marriage plans with latest hunky leading man...*

A white fury filled Lana. So *that* was what he'd done with *her* money! Taken it to Hollywood with him to splurge on his career.

She forced her fury down. What did it matter what Malcolm had blown her money on?

Giavanna was looking at her expectantly, and now Lana could not mistake the gleam of malice in her eyes. She would not rise to it, though.

'Mal moved on a long time ago,' she said dismissively.

'As did you,' came the reply.

'Indeed,' Lana replied evenly. 'As did I.'

She made some polite remark, wishing Giavanna all the best for her wedding, and then made her escape, getting into the car she had summoned from the boutique when she'd finished shopping.

That encounter with Giavanna had disturbed her tranquility, reminding her of a time in her life she didn't want to think about any longer, even though the ramifications of it—the crushing debt Mal's perfidy had dumped on her—still cast a long shadow.

But Mal himself was out of her life. Nothing left of him but a photo.

One day all I'll have of Salvatore will be photos. Photos and memories. Nothing more.

She felt a hollow inside her as she heard the words inside her head, and she gazed out of the car window at the streets of Rome going by, wanting only to forget them. Not wanting to ask herself why that was.

'I have to fly to Milan next week. Will you come with me? You could refresh your wardrobe,' Salvatore remarked.

They were back at the *palazzo*, and he was glad. It was cooler here, and he and Lana made good use of the pool. How long ago it seemed since he had first seen her spread-eagled on that lounger, showing him nearly all of her fabulous body for his delectation…

It hadn't been his to enjoy then. But now… His eyes went to her across the dinner table where they sat out on the terrace. Now she was most definitely his to enjoy. Her beauty was richer, and riper than ever. Her Italian diet was enhancing her beauty every day. There even seemed to be a glow about her…

'My wardrobe is bulging at the seams!' Lana answered him with a laugh. 'How long do you need to spend in Milan?'

'A few days, no more.' An idea struck him. 'We

could head for the Lakes—before the rains arrive in the autumn. How does that sound?'

'Better than Milan, I must say. To be honest,' she said, 'Milan doesn't really appeal—I've been there so often.'

'Join me on the last day, and then we can take off for the Lakes,' Salvatore said promptly. 'All we have to choose is which one. Como is the closest to Milan.'

'Como it is, then,' she smiled.

He smiled back warmly. It would be good to show Lana the Lakes. Have her at his side.

It's always good to be with her—to have her with me.

The thought in his head brought him the usual nod of satisfaction. But it was followed by another in its wake.

Will it always be good? And how long is 'always'? If you can get shot of Roberto in less time than you thought it would take, now that he's co-operating, what happens about Lana? You won't need her...

The question hung in his consciousness as his gaze rested on her. He set it aside. Reached for the wine bottle instead, refilling their glasses. Starting to tell her about Lake Como.

A much better subject to think about.

Lana walked into the pool house, pulling off her top as she did so. The heat was such that the only relief other than going indoors—which seemed a shame on such a lovely day—was the pool. She dropped her top on to the slatted wooden bench, peeled off her shorts and panties, reaching for her one-piece. She did not need to tan, she was quite brown enough—even her tummy.

She glanced down, frowning slightly. She had definitely become rounder and softer, since abandoning her low-calorie modelling diet. Salvatore was a big fan of her curvier figure, and she smiled reminiscently. He'd set off for Milan that morning, and she missed him already.

Perhaps she should have gone with him, even though Milan was not her favourite place—too many frenzied fashion shows. But spending some time at Lake Como sounded far more attractive. It would be their last chance to see the Lakes before autumn. And by spring she would be back in London.

Heaviness pressed at her. She did not want to think about the end of her time with Salvatore. Wanted only to go on enjoying this time with him. While she had him.

She shook her head to clear such pointless thoughts, tugging her swimsuit up her legs, over her hips and tummy. She had to stretch the fabric to do so, and looked down at herself again. The roundness of her tummy seemed accentuated, and she frowned again. She was definitely putting on weight—quite a lot, it seemed. She almost looked—

In mid-tug, she froze, eyes widening in shock. Something Laura had said to her that very first time she'd met Salvatore's friends was suddenly in her head.

'You won't ever get away with hiding even the tiniest baby bump!'

The words hung there, like a hammer suspended over her head. She was unable to un-hear them...

Instantly into her head came denial. No, of course she wasn't! She couldn't be. It was impossible. More than impossible.

Unthinkable.

Because it would change everything—everything!—between Salvatore and me...

Blindly, she pulled her clothes back on and walked back up to the *palazzo,* feeling her heart thudding in her chest. She had to know! She would go to a *farmacia*...buy at testing kit. Right now—this afternoon. Tension racked through her as she hurried indoors, seeing a maid, asking for a car to be brought round for her straight away.

I have to know. I have to know for certain. I just have to.

Salvatore put down his phone, frowning. Lana wasn't picking up. He texted her instead, saying he wanted to show her where they'd be staying on Lake Como, right at the lake's edge. She was going to be flying up to Milan tomorrow afternoon, and then they'd set off for the lake.

A bit less rustic than our last lakeside holiday!

He'd ended by attaching a photo of the luxury villa hotel with its ornate frontage and boat dock.

He waited for her reply. It did not come. He phoned

her again. No answer. Only voicemail. He left a message, asking her to phone him back.

After forty minutes of fruitless waiting, he phoned home. Spoke to his housekeeper.

'But the *signora* set out this morning to join you!' Signora Guardi told him. 'She said she wanted to surprise you—'

Salvatore froze.

CHAPTER ELEVEN

HER FLAT SMELT musty after so many months left empty. Mechanically, Lana went around opening windows to let in fresh air, despite the damp chill outside, flicking on the heating, filling the kettle. She was going through the motions, but inside she was collapsing. Less than twenty-four hours ago she had been at the *palazzo*. Staring at that plastic strip with a hollowing of her insides.

I thought it would reassure me—not devastate me!

She had felt panic wash over her, but had fought it back. Fought to retain control of herself. Fought to *think*…

And she had done that all evening—thinking and thinking and thinking, until her head ached with it. Every thought piercing her like the thrust of a knife.

She was pregnant. Something that she had never envisaged as even a possibility. And something she never, *never* would have wanted—for one stark, implacable reason.

Because it was not part of the deal. The deal she had

struck with Salvatore. The very simple, very unambig-
uous deal.

*I play the role of his wife—he pays off my mortgage
in our pre-planned divorce settlement.*

And the fact that playing the role of his wife had
turned into her having a searing affair with him
changed nothing! Nothing at all.

She'd paced her bedroom at the *palazzo*, back and
forth, trying to see it in another way. But it had been
impossible.

*He never signed up for this—me getting pregnant.
He never signed up to anything more than a year with
me.*

She'd gazed bleakly out of the darkened window,
seeing nothing of the night beyond, expression drawn.
A year was all he wanted—he'd been up-front, honest,
straight-up. That honesty of his—after Malcolm's lies
and deceit—was what she had valued so much in her
relationship with Salvatore. She had trusted him—and
he had trusted her. They had both known they would
abide by their agreement with each other. And so for
her to tell him now that she was carrying his child…

Her face contorted in misery.

*He'll think I did it deliberately—or carelessly. It
doesn't matter which because the effect will be the
same. He'll feel it's his obligation to stand by me—to
make our marriage last in a way he never intended it
to! It will chain him to me—chain him to a child he
never planned for. Chain him in this marriage when I
know how negatively he feels about marriage.*

How could she do that to him?

She couldn't—that was all. She just could not.

And so in the morning, after a sleepless night, her head still aching, she had made the only possible decision. She'd packed a suitcase as if she were intending Milan to be her destination, and to account for why she wanted to get to Pisa airport that morning had told the staff she was flying up a day early, to surprise Salvatore. Then she had taken the first flight to London.

It had been agony to do so.

Agony to leave Italy.

To force herself to do so.

To leave Salvatore.

To know I will never see him again—

She felt that agony again, now, as she stood in the kitchen of her flat, musty and empty and drear, a thousand miles away from where she longed to be, hearing the kettle come to the boil. Sightlessly staring at the mug she'd taken out of the cupboard, at the packet of fruit tea she'd opened, filled with misery and anguish, her face drawn and gaunt, she faced the truth about why it was such agony to have done what she had. Leave Salvatore. Faced the truth she had been trying to deny for so long now, all through those glorious sun-filled days with Salvatore, in the ecstasy of their passionate nights together.

I've fallen in love with him! With Salvatore.

Too late—oh, far too late—self-knowledge pierced her. Was that what she had feared all along? That she would not be able to stop herself falling in love with him?

Is that why I turned him down that first time we ever

*met? Why I wanted our marriage to be in name only?
Why I told him, that night when we'd come back from
Florence, that I could not let it be anything else, saying it was because he was going to pay off my mortgage that I could not let there be anything between us?*

And when she'd been able to resist him no longer,
when it had become impossible to say no to him, then...
oh, then she had known. She had kept reminding herself
that they must part at the pre-appointed time, that she
must hope for nothing more, must give nothing of herself, want nothing more from him than what they had.

In vain.

*I went and fell in love with him... Knowing that it
could come to nothing...*

Heaviness crushed her. And hopelessness.

Into her head came a memory from Rome, when
she had first arrived there. How glad she had been that
Malcolm had never broken her heart. And how she'd
known she must make sure that she never fell for a man
who did not return her feelings, who did not want to
make his life with her.

Yet I've done exactly that!

Salvatore had never asked for love, nor offered it,
and he would not welcome or want it any more than he
would their baby. A real marriage, let alone fatherhood,
had never been part of his plan. Just a year of her life,
a passionate affair—and nothing more.

She felt tears sting her eyes, heard his name a cry
of heartbreak on her lips...a heartbreak that nothing
could mend. For there was only one thing that she could
do—that must be done. Cost her what it might.

I have to set him free and never tell him why. It's all that I can do for him.

Her silence must be her gift—the only gift of love she could give him. And he had given her a gift too—a gift he would never know.

Instinctively, protectively, her hand splayed out over her rounding midriff, her eyes welling with tears. She had been given such a gift—the gift of new life, growing within her... But she was paying such a price for it. To have Salvatore's baby—but not Salvatore.

Her eyes closed in anguish and the pent-up tears seeped down her cheeks.

Unstoppable.

Salvatore stood in Lana's bedroom at the *palazzo*. His mother's room. Stared at the silver tray on the dressing table that had once been his mother's. Stared at the diamond ring lying on that silver tray, catching the sunlight from the window. The ring he had given the woman he had married. Who had now walked out on him, leaving her betrothal ring behind, just as she had left behind all the couture clothes she'd bought as his wife.

She had just...gone.

Why?

The question burned in him. She'd gone without warning, without explanation—without any reason! His calls to her had gone unanswered, gone to voicemail. She had never returned them, just as she had ignored his texts. There had been nothing—absolutely nothing.

Lana had not just disappeared—she had refused all contact.

Why?

The brutal question slammed again in his head. Why had she told his housekeeper she had decided to fly up to Milan to join him there and then, at Pisa airport, where she had been driven, had vanished into Departures. All contact lost.

He turned on his heel. There were no answers here. He drove to Rome, the devil on his tail, not wanting to be stuck in the middle of Tuscany. Had she returned to London? And if so, why?

When he was in Rome she made contact—but not with him. He got a call from his London lawyer, telling him she was filing for divorce and would not be taking a penny of their prenup agreement. Giving no reason for why she had left him as she had.

Frustration seized him, emotions writhed in him, but he did not know what they were—knew only that they were tormenting him like the biting of venomous snakes. He would fly to London, get answers from her—demand them!

But before he could book his flight he was given his answer. Courtesy of a visitor to his apartment in Rome—the very last person on earth he'd expected to see.

Giavanna.

Lana glanced one more time around the flat, checking everything was neat and tidy for the prospective purchaser about to look it over. She'd put it on the market the day after getting back to London—and already there was interest. She was relieved. She needed to sell as soon as possible, for the best price she could. Then she'd pay off the swingeing mortgage and head out of London with whatever was left.

She'd find somewhere to start over, where she'd stay for the rest of her life. Just her and her baby. The way it had to be. Living her life without Salvatore.

She tried to tell herself that her marriage—her time with Salvatore—would have ended anyway, just as Salvatore had planned. Her discovery that she was pregnant had only ended it sooner, that was all. But however much she told herself that, it made no difference to the pain she felt at losing him.

Yet she knew, with a chill inside her that ate into her bones, that a worse pain might have faced her. A worse destiny.

If I'd told him I was pregnant and he'd felt obliged to keep our marriage going, for then baby's sake, then—oh, dear God—I'd have ended up like his mother! Married to a man I loved—a man who did not love me...

It would have been worse than anything!

No... She felt her heart clench. This was the only way—selling up, clearing out. Making a new home for herself. A new life. In the time to come, in the long, long years ahead, her baby would be her comfort and her joy.

All that I'll have of Salvatore—

The sudden sound of the entry phone broke her stricken thoughts. With a start, she went out into the external hallway to admit the estate agent and her prospective buyer.

But as she pulled back the door she froze. It was the last man on earth she'd ever expected to see again.

Malcolm.

Salvatore climbed into the taxi at Heathrow and curtly gave the address, throwing himself back into his seat and yanking on the seat belt. The devil was driving him, he knew that, and had been since his return to the *palazzo* from Milan. But now the devil had pushed the accelerator button.

Courtesy of Giavanna.

He could still hear the false sympathy in her voice as she'd stood there in his apartment in a replay of her last visit. But this time her bombshell had not been that she wanted to marry him. It had been one that was still ripping his guts out.

'My poor Salva... I think I may know why Lana has left you. Take a look at this—'

She'd held out her phone to him and he'd seen the photo—a man he had not recognised—but the caption had made his identity clear.

Giavanna's falsely sympathetic voice had trilled in his ears.

'Hollywood gossip says it's all over between Lana's ex and the A-lister he hooked, so he's going back to London. Who knows? Maybe he wants to get back together with Lana...'

Denial stabbed in Salvatore.

No! He would not believe it! It was just Giavanna

making trouble, being vindictive! He would not believe that the reason Lana had left him was because she was rushing back to the man who had treated her so despicably!

Then his lawyer's words echoed in his head. Lana was refusing to take any of the money agreed in their prenup. Why would she do that? Unless—

Is Malcolm coming back to London to pay her back the money he took from her? And if he does will she forgive him? Take him back? Is it him she loves—has loved all along?

The thought was like icy water in his veins. He could feel it now, chilling him to the core, defying him not to believe what he so desperately hoped was just Giavanna's poison—what Lana herself would, surely, *por Dio!* prove was nothing but poison when he got the truth from her!

Of course she had never gone back to Malcolm!

And then she will come back to me! To me...

Emotions scythed within him, slicing and slicing at him. He could not name them, knew only that they were emotions he had never felt before—and that they were unbearable.

Agony.

The taxi ate up the miles into London, cutting through the streets towards Notting Hill, drawing up outside the white terraced house he remembered from so long ago, when he'd given Lana a lift back from the fashion show after-party. He moved to open the taxi door—then froze.

The front door was opening. Someone was coming out. Not Lana. A man with bleached blond hair, gleaming capped white teeth, a California tan, sauntering down the steps with a smile on his face that was a smirk of satisfaction. He walked by, taking no notice of the taxi at the kerbside.

A knife was skewering Salvatore. A knife coated with Giavanna's poison. Poison that was no lie but devastating truth. The evidence of his own eyes.

He slumped back in his seat, curtly ordering the taxi driver to drive on. Where, he didn't care.

Only blackness was in his heart.

Bleakness.

Lana carefully stepped into the shower, felt the warm water sluicing down over her. As she started to lather her hair she glanced down at her fast-growing bump. Memory stabbed at her of how she'd stood in the pool house at the *palazzo*, seeing her newly rounded figure.

So long ago now.

Summer was long gone. Autumn too. And by spring—

By spring I'll be preparing to receive my first visitors. Opening up for Easter. The start of the holiday season.

She hadn't moved to the seaside after all, but she wasn't that far away, in an attractive abbey town in Dorset, popular with tourists. The established B&B was an old, pretty stone cottage, part of a terrace in a quiet street, with hollyhocks in the garden and lavender along the path. She'd bought it after the rapid sale of her flat, and it was already well booked for next season. It would bring her in sufficient income, she reckoned, to make her living there financially viable.

A new start—a new life.

A new life that she would always have had. It had come sooner than she'd thought it would, but it would have come to the same thing anyway. That was what she kept having to remind herself. However painful it was to do so. Salvatore had had no objection to her leaving him as she had. Any hope that he might have not wanted her to leave had withered and died.

He's accepted that I simply ended the marriage earlier than we'd originally agreed, and thereby forfeited the prenup settlement. He hasn't objected. Hasn't tried to get in touch.

Because he didn't want her back. Was happy that she'd gone. Had ended it all sooner than planned. Their divorce was proceeding with no objections from Salvatore.

He doesn't miss me at all!

The cry was in her heart, but she crushed it back. She rinsed her hair, feeling her eyes stinging. It was the shampoo, that was all. Nothing more than that. Not tears—no, not tears.

There was no point in tears. No point in waking in the long reaches of the night, longing to feel arms around her, her own arms wrapped around Salvatore's strong body.

It was all over.

She turned off the water, reaching for her towel, wringing out her hair and stepping carefully out of the cubicle, wrapping herself in another voluminous towel.

Time to get on with things.

Time to get on with the rest of her life.

The life that would always have been waiting for me.

That was the only comfort she could take. And just one more thing other than that. One she had never looked to have but which had been given to her for all that by Salvatore himself. His beloved child, growing within her.

Salvatore jabbed at the channel changing button on the remote, indifferent to what programme he might watch. It would pass the time. Maybe make the long, empty evening which stretched ahead of him pass less agonisingly slowly than they always did now.

He should go and get some work done. That would blot up more time. Time that stretched endlessly now, whatever he did.

He no longer went out. The sympathy of his friends was unbearable. Even the Duchessa had written to him, expressing her regret at hearing that he and Lana were divorcing.

She was good for you, Salvatore, and I know how much your mother would have approved of your marriage, rejoicing that you had found such happiness. My heart goes out to you that you have lost it now—lost Lana...

He had thrown the letter aside, not wanting to read it. Not wanting to hear what his mother's godmother had thought of his marriage…that she believed his mother would have approved of it.

He wanted to laugh—savagely. In a bitter mocking of himself.

He reached for the bottle of *grappa* sitting by his elbow, refilled the glass he had already emptied. It did not help him—did not ease the hyenas tearing at his guts as they so ceaselessly did.

His eyes were bloodshot—and as bleak as polar ice.

He jabbed again at the remote, staring sightlessly at the huge screen over the fireplace. Some pointless documentaries, some pointless advertisements, some pointless programme about new film releases…

He let that last one settle, running out of programmes to surf. It finished by waxing lyrical about some new pointless blockbuster, then went on to something about a pointless Hollywood wedding…

And suddenly Salvatore straightened from his slump on the sofa, his eyes no longer bloodshot or bleak, but focussed, like a laser beam on what he was seeing.

As the item ended on a saccharine gush, in slow motion he set down his undrunk *grappa*. Got to his feet. Swayed slightly and then, with the force of will, straightened.

He had to sober up. And fast.

He had a flight to book.

Lana unpacked the groceries she'd just bought, neatly placing them in the kitchen cupboards. Memory stabbed at her of how she and Salvatore had unpacked their provisions in the lakeside cabin. She put the memory aside. Put them all aside. One day she would let them out. Tell her son or daughter as they grew up about the father they would never know.

Never could know.

She must not long for anything else.

I must not long for him with all my heart, with all that I feel for him. That is so, so hopeless! So pointless!

Yet memory came again, and she was lost in that unforgettable time with Salvatore at the lakeside cabin, out on the lake in the little rowing boat, as she'd asked about how he'd come to love fishing, and he'd told her about his father…about his indifference to his wife's love for him.

'He never wanted a divorce—he stayed with her for my sake…'

Pain twisted like a knife in her side.

That would have been her fate, too, had she told Salvatore about the baby. And it would have tortured her to know how much she loved him—and how indifferent to her he would have become when his desire for her finally died. He would have resented being married to her—or, worse, agreed to some 'civilised' divorce, some 'civilised' arrangement over shared custody and access…

Unbearable—just unbearable—

The knife twisted again, but she stifled the pain. There was no point feeling it—no point at all. It would be there all her life, she knew.

Her life without Salvatore…

Whom she would never see again…

Never.

The word tolled like a funeral bell in her head.

Then, as if thought had become reality, she heard the front doorbell ring. She started, wondering who was there—a late postal delivery, perhaps? She went to the door, opened it, blinking in the wintry sunlight that caught her eyes. Silhouetting the man standing there.

'Never' had been the wrong word. So she said his name instead, in a breathy gasp, as all the air left her lungs.

'Salvatore...'

CHAPTER TWELVE

HE STOOD THERE, motionless, for an endless moment.

Lana! I am seeing her again—here, now, in front of me!

She overwhelmed him, making his senses reel.

But she always had—she had always had that effect on him. From the very first moment to the very last.

His gaze swept over her. He was drinking her in like a man in a desert finding sweet, sweet water...

He looked her over from her golden hair, piled up loosely, to her perfect face—perfect even without make-up, for it was always perfect, could only ever be perfect—down over her fabulous body—

And stopped short.

'Dio mio...'

The breath was exhaled from him and shock—naked and brutal—punched him in the solar plexus. Her pregnancy was blatant—unconcealed. The long sweater over leggings outlined her fullness.

Shock detonated in him again as he took it in.

He heard her say his name, shock whitening her face. Saw her slump against the door...

In an instant he had her, catching her before she fell. The weight of her body was heavy—heavier than he had ever known it. But then...

'You need to sit down.' His voice was brusque, terse with shock. Inside his head emotion was storming.

He guided her in, kicking the door shut behind him, going into a room opening off the hallway. It was a sitting room, warm from central heating after the chill of the English winter outdoors, and he got her to an armchair into which she sank like a dead weight.

He heard her say his name again, in the same faint voice, her eyes huge in her head, still blank with shock. Emotion was storming within him, and seeing her in that condition was like being inside a hurricane, turning him inside out. Everything he had come here to say vanished from him, torn away by the storm whipping through him.

He stood back, looking down at her. Then spoke, finding the necessary words. 'Let me get you some water—'

His voice was clipped, and he did not wait for a reply, just strode from the room. Behind the sitting room was a kitchen, and he seized up a glass from the draining board, filling it from the tap, coming back into the room where Lana still sat, her face ashen.

'Drink this,' he told her, handing her the glass.

She took it, sipping from it jerkily until he removed it again, setting it down on a nearby side table.

Then he stood, looking down at her. The hurricane was still inside him, or he was inside it—he did not know. But he was calmer now, forcing himself to be so. Finding the words he knew he now must say.

He drew breath, steadying his voice. But it still came out harshly. 'I should hate you for what you did to me—leaving me as you did, and for such a reason. But now—'

He stopped. She was staring at him, her beautiful face still ashen. Something moved within him, crossing the whipping maelstrom of the hurricane inside him and finding the still, small eye where the maelstrom could not reach. Where he now was. Where everything was clear to him.

'I will stand by you,' he said. He drew a breath, like a razor in his throat, ready to say what he must say next, where only truth could be.

When he spoke again his eyes never left hers. His voice was no longer harsh. It was filled, instead, with all he knew he must say to her.

'Come back to me, Lana. It's what I came here to say to you…'

He had known it from the moment he'd realised that whatever kind of reunion she'd had with Malcolm it was over—he'd gone back to Hollywood to marry a film star. Leaving Lana alone. Alone for him to say what he had just said to her.

His eyes went to her midriff and emotion knifed within him. Emotion that filled him with a certainty that made everything else irrelevant. For a moment there was silence, only the ticking of a clock on the mantelpiece making any sound. Yet his heart was pounding such that surely it must be audible. As audible as the words echoing in his head now. The words he had said.

No man in his right mind would say them. What man could? In his head a memory flashed—seared—of his talking to Luc Dinardi about Stephanie. It had been unbelievable then, what Luc had said. But now—

Now I know. Know why he would say it. And why I have said it too.

And he knew why the words he would speak now were the only ones he wanted to say. Spoken out of that still, small space inside the hurricane where truth was. The only truth that mattered.

The certainty of it poured through him and his gaze poured into hers as she stared up at him, uncomprehending, stricken…

'I will stand by you,' he said, with indelible certainty, absolute promise. 'And I give you my word…' his eyes held all that he knew he must say '…no one will ever know your baby is not mine.'

Lana lurched to her feet and the blood drained from her again, making her legs collapse, her lungs collapse. For a second time Salvatore caught her, his hands gripping hers as her body sagged.

'No, don't faint on me! I didn't mean to shock you! Sit down—'

Once again he was propelling her into the armchair and she sank down. If she had been in shock before, now it was threefold. A million-fold. He let slip her hands and they dropped like weights into her lap as he stood there, looking down at her.

What was in his face was something she had never seen before.

He was speaking again, and in his voice was something she had never heard before.

'I do not talk of forgiveness,' he was saying, his eyes never leaving hers, 'for there is nothing to forgive. You knew him before you knew me. He hurt you badly and you hated him for it! So I understand—truly, I understand why you went back to him when he returned to London. And I understand your hopes, your thinking—believing—he might stay with you this time...'

And now his voice darkened, edged with an anger, a contempt, that was not directed at her.

'But you were wrong to trust him—he let you down again! Abandoned you again! Used you just as he used you the first time around!' His eyes flashed with anger. 'If he were here now I would pulverise him for what he's done to you! Left you—again! Looking out for himself, and only for himself, as he always did!'

She couldn't speak...couldn't think. Could not believe—

But he was not done yet.

'For all that he has done to you, you are well shot of him! He's worthless scum! Forget him! Forget him and come back to me.'

She took a breath. Deep into her lungs. Her whole being seemed to be sucked into that breath. She looked up at him. She couldn't read his face. It had closed again.

'Are you telling me,' she asked slowly, with infinite care—because suddenly, out of nowhere, out of the maelstrom that had stormed over her, it was the most important question in the world, in the entire universe, '—that you would want me even if I was carrying Malcolm's baby?'

His eyes were fixed on hers. His face still had that expression she had never seen before, the one that was impossible to read.

'Yes.'

A single word to answer her.

She took a ragged breath. It seemed the words must break from her now.

'But *why*?'

For a moment he did not answer her. Only stood there, his gaze still fixed on hers. That unreadable look still on his face. She felt her heart start to thud, as if something were about to happen that she might not be able to bear.

She could see the tension edging his jaw, sitting across his shoulders, when he spoke next, as if his words were being forced from him. She heard them through the thudding of her heart, the tightness in her lungs. Sitting there, nerveless.

'All my life,' he said heavily, 'I have thought myself like my father. Feared it. I knew, therefore, that I should never marry lest I bring misery to my wife as he did to his. But then I discovered something about myself that I had never known,' he said, and his words were heavier yet. 'Giavanna came to see me after you'd walked out on me. Dropping poison in my ear. Giving me an explanation for why you'd left me. *Por Dio*, I did not believe it—did not want to believe it! Refused to believe it! Yet when I came to your house and saw Malcolm walking out of it…then I knew—'

Pain was in his voice—she could hear it through the thudding of her heart—and a hurt and wretchedness that reached out to her and gripped her heart like a vice.

'I knew, in that single moment, that it was not being my father's son that I should have feared…' He looked at her, and the pain that had been in his voice was in his eyes too. 'It was being my mother's.'

He was silent for a moment, and so was she, unable to speak, too full with what was inside her now. Then more words were coming from Salvatore. Halting, painful.

'I had come to know, as she did, the pain of being rejected for another. Because you…' his face was bleaker yet '…had rejected me for Malcolm, who wanted you back after he'd been dumped by his Hollywood star.'

Slowly…infinitely slowly…Lana found the words she needed to speak. 'How could you *ever* think I would go back to Malcolm? After what he did to me!'

The tightness of his face made it a mask. 'I thought he must have repented…repaid you the mortgage money.' His mouth set. 'I thought that that was the reason you were turning down the prenup payment we'd agreed.'

Lana's eyes widened in disbelief. 'I refused to take your money because I'd broken the terms of our deal! I'd left you before the year was out. That was why!'

She felt her face work. Thoughts, feelings, emotions, words were tumbling within her, but she must make sense of them—she *must*. And above all she must say what she had to now.

'I *never* left you for Malcolm—even though, yes, he did repay what he owed me! You saw him leave my flat,' she said, her voice hollow, 'because he'd been sent there by his fiancée—who hadn't dumped him, whatever the gossip said! She discovered that I'd claimed he'd defrauded me, that I was seeking to press charges. She didn't want any scandal attached to him so she sent him there, gave him the money to repay the mortgage, in exchange for dropping all my accusations. Which I did.'

Salvatore was staring at her. Something different in his face now. 'So you got your money back, and you slept with him one last time, for old times' sake?'

There was no expression in his voice.

Nor was there in Lana's as she answered him.

'No,' she said again. 'It wasn't like that, Salvatore.'

She made herself look at him. The thud of her heart was deafening her. She gave a cry. Launching herself to her feet.

'Why do you think I left you?'

The words broke from her—impossible to halt them, to silence them, to keep them locked within her any longer. Not a second longer. It was no longer possible to keep hidden the truth she'd had to hide.

He stilled. Utterly motionless.

'I left you because I found out I was pregnant,' she said, and each word was forced from her. They were the most important, the most vital words she would ever utter in her life, and her whole life now depended on them. 'And when I did, I knew I could not impose upon you what you had never agreed to. What broke our agreement into pieces. It…it would not have been fair on you.'

She took a breath before plunging on, saying what must be said—what could not be left unsaid. They had gone way beyond that now.

'You were always honest with me, Salvatore…' Her voice changed as she spoke now, and her eyes echoed the truth of what she was saying. 'Honest about the reasons we married, about when it would end, and why— honest when you said that we would only have a year together…honest about what you felt for me. Desire, yes, but nothing more. And, wonderful though our time was—and I am joyously glad that we had what we had together, and it felt right to be with you and to want you, be wanted by you—for all that… I always knew I was on borrowed time. That we would part.'

She shook her head.

'There was nothing…nothing that gave me any claim on anything else from you. Like…like being pregnant. So,' she finished, 'because of that I knew I could only do what I did. I left you. And although I would have given all the world not to have had to leave you, it was as simple as that.'

She fell silent, but she could hear each beat of her heart, each pulse of her blood.

'And when you did…when you left me,' he answered her, 'my world ended. It was as simple as that. And devastating to me.'

He shut his eyes for a moment, then they flashed

open again, gold blazing in their night-dark depths. Gold that could melt her where she stood.

He took a step towards her. Halted. 'When I married you, Lana, I did so for hard-headed reasons—and I was honest with you, as you say, from the off. I wanted nothing more than what I'd planned—a year with you, no more.' He drew a razoring breath. 'I've never done long relationships because...' The razoring breath came again. 'Because I never...*never*...wanted to cause any woman the misery my mother endured because of my father. The father I thought I was like. *Feared* I was like...'

He was silent a moment, his face drawn. Then he spoke again, and now there was something different about him. Something clearer in his eyes.

'I thought all I wanted of you was an affair—that it would end like all my affairs end. That the time would come when I would stop wanting you, as has always been the case with me—as it was for my father. But it took your leaving—leaving me for another man, as I so insanely thought—to make me realise something that I had never known...something only the agony I felt when you left me could show me.'

He took a breath, but this time it was not razoring at all. Only resolute. As resolute as his voice when he spoke to her again.

'Show me,' he said, his eyes holding hers as if they were precious jewels he must never lose. 'Show me that I am not my father's son, Lana, but that I am my mother's. And that as my mother's son I can know—as I did not when I thought I was like my father, incapable

of emotional attachment—that all the time we were
together I was falling in love with you, even though I
had no idea of it.'

He took a breath from the very depths of his being,
his eyes pouring into hers with such intensity that she
reeled from it.

He shook his head. 'I did not know it…did not recognise it. But now…' He took another, deeper breath,
his eyes still pouring into hers. 'Now I do recognise
it—I know it for what it is. And even if it's only the
sake of the baby…' his voice was diffident now, hesi-
tant, unsure '…if you will come back to me, then—'

She cut across him instinctively, her words as heartfelt as everything that was in her. 'Then I will have
found my paradise, Salvatore.'

She took a step towards him, reached out her hands
to him. Her heart was singing, soaring to the very heavens.

'Oh, my most dearest one, I have known I loved you
ever since I left you. It nearly killed me to have to leave
you!' Her voice twisted, emotion breaking in it. 'But
when I discovered I was pregnant I could not bear to
make you resent me, make you feel that I was trapping
you! I knew, for your sake, that I could not tell you I
was pregnant! I could not do that to you. Not for your
sake, Salvatore, or—' her voice broke '—or for mine.'

The words poured from her—all that had been stifled, all that she had not been allowed to say but now
she could. She could speak at last.

'You say you are your mother's son—but, oh, Salvatore, I feared I, too, would be like your mother! Feared

it for myself! Feared loving you so much and you never loving me—never wanting my love, never giving me yours, only staying with me for the sake of our child. I could not bear it! I knew I'd rather live out my life alone than that!'

He seized her hands, closing the distance between them. Clasping her fingers so tightly it was as if he would fuse flesh with flesh.

'And I knew,' he said, and there was something in his voice she had never heard there before, something that pierced her to the core, 'that loving you so much, as I do, I would rather have you in my life with another man's baby than not have you in it at all.'

She gave a little cry, unbearably moved, and lifted his hand to her cheek. 'If ever I wanted proof of your love, that declaration would be it! Oh, my darling, my dearest love—'

Tears were welling in her eyes, misting her face. He bent his face to hers, to kiss away the tears, and lowered his hand so that he could embrace her, hold her close against him.

For ever.

Then suddenly she gave a little cry, pulling back from him.

Consternation immediately filled Salvatore's face. 'Lana—no, don't pull away. Please—don't pull away from me! Not when I love you so much!'

She heard those words, so very dear to her, from this man who had once only wanted her for a year, no more than that, but who would now be hers, as she was his, for ever! Her hand had gone to the swell of her body, splaying over it. She lifted her face lifted to Salvatore's, amazement and wonder in her eyes, joy coursing through every atom of her being after his declaration of love for her.

'He moved! Salvatore, he *moved*! I felt him just now! Like a butterfly inside me!' She gave another cry, a gasp. 'And again! He moved again. Oh, Salvatore…'

She reached for his hand, placed it next to hers, radiant joy in her face. And not just for the baby quickening within her—but for all the joy that was pouring through her now. And for ever and ever.

She saw his expression change, saw the same look of wonder in his eyes as in hers, heard him give the same gasp of breath.

'Si—il muovo!'

For a moment longer they just stood there, as the child they had created between them made its presence felt. Then Salvatore's free hand cupped her face. His eyes poured into hers, telling her, without words, of his love for her. Telling her that her joy was his as well.

'It's a wise child that knows his own father,' he told her, and there was a catch in his voice that turned her heart over.

She gave a cry of laughter, but there were tears in her voice as well. Laughter, and tears, and a joy that could light up the world.

For both of them.

'And it's an even wiser father,' Salvatore went on, catching Lana back into his arms, 'who knows with every atom of his being that he is in love with the woman who is the beloved mother of his most precious baby.'

He kissed her then, and in his lips and hers was all she could ever have desired and dreamt of.

He held her in the cradle of his arms as he released her. His eyes held hers, glinting gold in the noonday light.

'I have a new business proposition to put to you, Signora Luchesi,' he said. 'I don't think a year of marriage is anything like enough. So I'm revising the end date of our contract.' His mouth skimmed hers, taking sweet possession, just to remind her, as her hands wound around his waist, of her possession of him too. 'I am setting it for a hundred years from now. 'That should be sufficient, I think,' he told her, kissing the tip of her nose, and then her forehead.

She shook her head. 'Let's go for broke,' she said, lifting her mouth to claim his again. 'Let's go for eternity.'

His arms tightened around her. 'Eternity it is, then,' he said. 'Sounds good to me.'

'And to me,' she whispered.

Their kiss deepened, and then, with an effortless swing of his arms, Salvatore was sweeping her up.

'This is a delightful cottage,' he informed her, with purpose in his voice, 'but right now there is only one room I want to find.'

She laughed, carefree in her whole being, as she would always be now. 'Upstairs, first on the right. And you'll be glad to know,' she said, eyes gleaming, 'that it's a king-size bed.'

She was right. Salvatore was very glad.

And so, she found, to her satisfaction, delight and incandescent joy, was she, as with all their passion and desire they proved their newly declared love for each other.

EPILOGUE

LANA STOOD BESIDE Salvatore, her emerald silk evening gown brushing the smooth black of his evening jacket, leaning against him as they both gazed down at the sleeping baby in his cot.

'He is simply the most perfect baby that ever there was!' Lana breathed, her gaze filled with devoted love.

Salvatore's arm came around her waist. 'Absolutely the most perfect,' he agreed.

For a few moments longer they stood there, gazing down in joint admiration of the son, who had been born in the early summer. Now it was August, and the *palazzo*, ablaze with lights, was preparing to receive its guests for the summer ball that was to take place that night. Already, through the open windows, they could hear the strains of the orchestra tuning up on the terrace, now bedecked with fairy lights, and the bustle of the staff as they made everything ready for the glittering occasion.

First, though, Lana and Salvatore were dining with their closest friends, who were staying with them at the *palazzo*.

Salvatore led Lana downstairs from the nursery, leaving their precious son in the reassuring charge of Signora Guardi's niece, who would babysit for the evening.

In the *saloni* opposite the dining room Giuseppe was opening the champagne, and Lana paused to thank and praise him and all the staff for their efforts tonight. He bestowed a smile upon her, and Lana returned it warmly. Now she truly felt herself the chatelaine of this beautiful *palazzo*, she thought fondly, her eyes going to Salvatore, the man who was the love of her life. It was her home for ever, and she was no longer the imposter she had thought herself when she'd first come here, uneasy at being treated as the *signora* and successor to Salvatore's mother.

Now I truly belong here!

It was a good feeling—a wonderful feeling…

The arrival of her and Salvatore's dinner guests into the *saloni* drew her attention. Laura and Stephanie—both, like Lana, dressed to the nines in couture gowns and diamond jewellery—hugged Lana, and then Vito and Luc, as resplendent as Salvatore in their evening dress, bestowed hand kisses with Latin gallantry. As the champagne circulated Lana was filled with a happiness that permeated every cell of her body. How happy she was…how perfectly, absolutely happy!

Lana's smile radiated from her and Salvatore's breath caught, his gaze fastening on her, his heart turning over with all that he felt for her. His Lana! His wonderful, beautiful Lana! His very own most beloved of women.

My wife.

His true wife—his one and only wife—his one and only love.

He closed his eyes for a moment. Had he really once thought it was impossible to fall in love, to want to spend all his days—and, oh, all his nights!—with one woman and one alone? Had he really thought that? Now every day, every night, every waking moment gave the lie to that.

Quietly, blinking suddenly, he raised his glass a little. Giving a silent toast.

But, slight though the gesture had been Lana caught it.

She met his eyes. 'How right she was,' she said softly, for him alone.

She knew what he was doing, and why, as the others chatted amongst themselves, laughing with the conviviality of good friends.

'Your mother knew you better than you knew yourself.'

She kissed him lightly on his cheek and he caught her hand, pressing it.

'And how happy she would be, seeing you so happy.' She paused for a moment. 'And I think, too, you know, that your father would be happy as well, knowing you have found a happiness in marriage that he never did.'

She bit her lip for a moment, throat tightening.

'One day you'll be taking *your* son off fishing, telling him how your father taught you and now you're teaching him.'

Salvatore smiled. 'It will be a year or two yet, I think. And who knows…?'

A sudden glint lit his deep, dark, long-lashed eyes, sweeping over Lana in a way she knew only too well. She felt her whole body quiver, the way it always did when he looked at her like that.

'Perhaps by then he'll have a younger brother for me to teach to fish as well.'

'Or a sister,' Lana said.

'Or a sister,' Salvatore agreed.

He raised his glass again, to her, his beloved wife. 'To our children and to us—and to our parents too.'

His gaze widened, taking in his friends.

'And to our friends!' He raised his voice and his glass.

Contentment filled him. Could life be better? He doubted it. He had his beloved wife, his adored son, and his beautiful home—created by his mother, purchased thanks to his father's business acumen. He had his health and his career—and his friends. And all the guests who would come later that evening.

The Duchessa and her husband would be there, bestowing their approval upon his renewed and so obviously happy marriage. And even Roberto would be there too. He gave a wry smile. They were on good terms now, with Roberto basking in his daughter's marriage into the aristocracy and Giavanna preening happily with her *visconte* heir.

'To friendship!' Vito echoed Salvatore's toast.

'Brava!' cried Steph enthusiastically. 'And,' she added, pausing for dramatic effect, to ensure she had all eyes on her, 'to one thing more!' She glanced at Luc, who smiled down at her indulgently.

'Go on,' he said. 'You can be the very first to announce this prime morsel of gossip, my treasure!'

Stephanie's eyes sparkled with delight. 'Then I shall!' She took another dramatic breath. 'I've decided, after *long* consideration, that it's high time I made an honest man out of Rome's favourite playboy. So...' She raised her glass. 'I hereby announce that Luc Dinardi is being taken out of circulation, to the tears and lamentations of all females everywhere, and is about to become my true and faithful husband. *Because*...'

She paused again, and exchanged a wicked glance with Laura and with Lana, who both silently gasped, as if they knew exactly what their incorrigible friend was going to announce, and that Luc had absolutely no idea of it.

'Because he's going to be a father too!'

A shout of delight broke from both Salvatore and Vito, followed by the back-slapping of a somewhat stunned-looking Luc.

His new fiancée patted him comfortingly on the wrist. 'Yes, Luc—and, yes, the baby *is* yours. Would I even dream of having a baby with anyone but you, my own beloved man of mine! How could you ever think such a thing of me?' she added demurely.

Salvatore and Lana exchanged glances and she felt him take her hand in hers, squeezing it. Both of them remembered how Salvatore had, in one heartfelt assurance, declared the extent of his love for her. Lana felt her eyes fill with tears now, at the very memory. How foolish she had been to think she must flee from Salvatore, to think he would not welcome their child!

And how glorious had been the realisation of just how much he loved her!

Her fingers tightened on his as she gazed at him, lovelight lambent in her eyes, glowing like the emerald silk of her gown. And for a moment…a timeless, eternal moment…there was no one else in the room, no one else in the whole world except herself—and the man she loved.

For all eternity.

Then, as Salvatore's mouth swooped down to steal a swift, infinitely tender kiss, the world returned.

Vito was raising his glass. His sweeping gaze encompassing them all. 'The toast, my friends, is to love, marriage—and babies!'

It was a toast they could all drink to.

So they did.

* * * * *

If you fell in love with
Destitute Until the Italian's Diamond
then you'll be head over heels for
these other stories by Julia James!

Irresistible Bargain with the Greek
The Greek's Duty-Bound Royal Bride
The Greek's Penniless Cinderella
Cinderella in the Boss's Palazzo
Cinderella's Baby Confession

Available now!

#4033 THE SECRET THAT SHOCKED CINDERELLA
by Maisey Yates
Riot wakes from a coma with no recollection of Kravann, the brooding fiancé at her bedside, *or* her baby! Her amnesia has given Kravann a second chance. Can he get their whirlwind love affair right this time?

#4034 EMERGENCY MARRIAGE TO THE GREEK
by Clare Connelly
Tessa returns to billionaire Alexandros's life with an outrageous emergency request—for his ring! But if he's going to consider her proposal, he has some conditions of his own: a *real* marriage...and an heir!

#4035 STOLEN FOR MY SPANISH SCANDAL
Rival Billionaire Tycoons
by Jackie Ashenden
My reunion with my stepbrother Constantine Silvera resulted in an explosion of forbidden, utterly unforgettable passion...leaving me pregnant! The Spaniard is determined to claim our child. So now here I am, unceremoniously kidnapped and stranded in his beautiful manor house!

#4036 WILLED TO WED HIM
by Caitlin Crews
To save her family legacy, her father's will demands that Annika wed superrich yet intimidating Ranieri. She knows he's marrying her in cold blood, but behind the doors of his Manhattan penthouse, he ignites a fire in her she never dreamed possible...

#4037 INNOCENT UNTIL HIS FORBIDDEN TOUCH
Scandalous Sicilian Cinderellas
by Carol Marinelli

PR pro Beatrice's brief is simple—clean up playboy prince Julius's image before he becomes king. A challenge made complicated by the heat she feels for her off-limits client! For the first time, innocent Beatrice *wants* to give in to wild temptation...

#4038 THE DESERT KING MEETS HIS MATCH
by Annie West

Sheikh Salim needs a wife—immediately! But when he's introduced to matchmaker Rosanna, he's hit with a red-hot jolt of recognition... Because she's the fiery stranger from an electric encounter he *never* forgot!

#4039 CLAIMED TO SAVE HIS CROWN
The Royals of Svardia
by Pippa Roscoe

After lady-in-waiting Henna stops a marriage that would protect King Aleks's throne, he's furious. Until a transformational kiss awakens him to a surprising new possibility that could save his crown... And it starts with *her*!

#4040 THE POWERFUL BOSS SHE CRAVES
Scandals of the Le Roux Wedding
by Joss Wood

Event planner Ella is done with men who call the shots. So when commanding Micah requests her expertise for his sister's society wedding, she can't believe she's considering it. Only there's something about her steel-edged new boss that intrigues and attracts Ella beyond reason...

YOU CAN FIND MORE INFORMATION ON UPCOMING HARLEQUIN TITLES, FREE EXCERPTS AND MORE AT HARLEQUIN.COM.

HPCNMRB0722

*My reunion with my stepbrother Constantin Silvera
resulted in an explosion of forbidden, utterly
unforgettable passion...leaving me pregnant! The
Spaniard is determined to claim our child. So now
here I am, unceremoniously kidnapped and stranded
in his beautiful manor house!*

*Read on for a sneak preview of
Jackie Ashenden's next story for Harlequin Presents*
Stolen for My Spanish Scandal

Constantin's black winged brows drew down very
slightly. "So, you haven't come here to tell me?"

Cold swept through me, my gut twisting and making
me feel even more ill. I put a hand on the back of the
uncomfortable couch, steadying myself, because he
couldn't know. He couldn't. I'd told no one. It was my
perfect little secret and that was how I'd wanted it to
stay.

"Tell you?" I tried to sound as innocent as possible,
to let my expression show nothing but polite inquiry.

"Tell you what?"

His inky brows twitched as he looked down at me from his great height, his beautiful face as expressive as a mountainside. "That you're pregnant, of course."

Don't miss
Stolen for My Spanish Scandal,
available September 2022 wherever
Harlequin Presents books and ebooks are sold.

Harlequin.com

Get 4 FREE REWARDS!

We'll send you 2 FREE Books plus 2 FREE Mystery Gifts.

FREE Value Over **$20**

Both the **Harlequin® Desire** and **Harlequin Presents®** series feature compelling novels filled with passion, sensuality and intriguing scandals.

YES! Please send me 2 FREE novels from the Harlequin Desire or Harlequin Presents series and my 2 FREE gifts (gifts are worth about $10 retail). After receiving them, if I don't wish to receive any more books, I can return the shipping statement marked "cancel." If I don't cancel, I will receive 6 brand-new Harlequin Presents Larger-Print books every month and be billed just $5.80 each in the U.S. or $5.99 each in Canada, a savings of at least 11% off the cover price or 6 Harlequin Desire books every month and be billed just $4.55 each in the U.S. or $5.24 each in Canada, a savings of at least 13% off the cover price. It's quite a bargain! Shipping and handling is just 50¢ per book in the U.S. and $1.25 per book in Canada.* I understand that accepting the 2 free books and gifts places me under no obligation to buy anything. I can always return a shipment and cancel at any time. The free books and gifts are mine to keep no matter what I decide.

Choose one: ☐ **Harlequin Desire**
(225/326 HDN GNND)

☐ **Harlequin Presents Larger-Print**
(176/376 HDN GNWY)

Name (please print)

Address   Apt. #

City   State/Province   Zip/Postal Code

Email: Please check this box ☐ if you would like to receive newsletters and promotional emails from Harlequin Enterprises ULC and its affiliates. You can unsubscribe anytime.

Mail to the **Harlequin Reader Service:**
IN U.S.A.: P.O. Box 1341, Buffalo, NY 14240-8531
IN CANADA: P.O. Box 603, Fort Erie, Ontario L2A 5X3

Want to try 2 free books from another series? Call 1-800-873-8635 or visit www.ReaderService.com.

*Terms and prices subject to change without notice. Prices do not include sales taxes, which will be charged (if applicable) based on your state or country of residence. Canadian residents will be charged applicable taxes. Offer not valid in Quebec. This offer is limited to one order per household. Books received may not be as shown. Not valid for current subscribers to the Harlequin Presents or Harlequin Desire series. All orders subject to approval. Credit or debit balances in a customer's account(s) may be offset by any other outstanding balance owed by or to the customer. Please allow 4 to 6 weeks for delivery. Offer available while quantities last.

Your Privacy—Your information is being collected by Harlequin Enterprises ULC, operating as Harlequin Reader Service. For a complete summary of the information we collect, how we use this information and to whom it is disclosed, please visit our privacy notice located at corporate.harlequin.com/privacy-notice. From time to time we may also exchange your personal information with reputable third parties. If you wish to opt out of this sharing of your personal information, please visit readerservice.com/consumerschoice or call 1-800-873-8635. **Notice to California Residents**—Under California law, you have specific rights to control and access your data. For more information on these rights and how to exercise them, visit corporate.harlequin.com/california-privacy.

HDHP22